[illegible] TO READERS

[illegible] book [illegible]

[illegible] ULVERSCROFT FOUNDATION

[illegible] charity [illegible] No. [illegible]

The Foundation [illegible] are [illegible] diagnosis and treatment of eye diseases. [illegible] examples [illegible] made by the ULVERSCROFT FOUNDATION [illegible]

A new Children's Assessment Unit at Moorfield's Hospital, London.

•

Twin operating theatres at the Western Ophthalmic Hospital, London.

•

The Frederick Thorpe Ulverscroft Chair of Ophthalmology at the University of Leicester.

•

Eye Laser equipment to various eye hospitals.

If you would like [illegible] the work of the Foundation by [illegible] legacy [illegible] contribution [illegible] details [illegible]

THE ULVERSCROFT FOUNDATION,

The Green, Bradgate Road, Anstey,

Leicester LE7 7FU. England.

Telephone: (0533) 364 [illegible]

SPECIAL MESSAGE TO READERS

This book is published by
THE ULVERSCROFT FOUNDATION
a registered charity in the U.K., No. 264873

The Foundation was established in 1974 to provide funds to help towards research, diagnosis and treatment of eye diseases. Below are a few examples of contributions made by THE ULVERSCROFT FOUNDATION:

A new Children's Assessment Unit at Moorfield's Hospital, London.

•

Twin operating theatres at the Western Ophthalmic Hospital, London.

•

The Frederick Thorpe Ulverscroft Chair of Ophthalmology at the University of Leicester.

•

Eye Laser equipment to various eye hospitals.

If you would like to help further the work of the Foundation by making a donation or leaving a legacy, every contribution, no matter how small, is received with gratitude. Please write for details to:

THE ULVERSCROFT FOUNDATION,
The Green, Bradgate Road, Anstey,
Leicester LE7 7FU. England
Telephone: (0533)364325

ONE HELL OF A SHOWDOWN

The mixed half dozen — Larry and Stretch, Nevada Jim and Benito, Doc Beaumont and Slow Wolf — join forces again in pursuit of a vengeance-crazed killer and his ten unsavoury cohorts. The hunt began in North Nevada and ended in a dying Colorado town, and the end was violent, a never-to-be-forgotten fight to the finish.

MARSHALL GROVER

ONE HELL OF A SHOWDOWN

A Larry & Stretch Western

Complete and Unabridged

LINFORD
Leicester

First published in Australia in 1990 by
Horwitz Grahame Pty Limited
Australia

First Linford Edition
published December 1993
by arrangement with
Horwitz Grahame Pty Limited
Australia

British Library CIP Data

Grover, Marshall
One hell of a showdown.—Large print ed.—
Linford western library
I. Title II. Series
823 [F]

ISBN 0-7089-7448-1

Published by
F. A. Thorpe (Publishing) Ltd.
Anstey, Leicestershire

Set by Words & Graphics Ltd.
Anstey, Leicestershire
Printed and bound in Great Britain by
T. J. Press (Padstow) Ltd., Padstow, Cornwall

This book is printed on acid-free paper

Dedicated to my father
FRANCIS EDWIN MEARES
Musician, barber and
quite a yarn-spinner

1

The Grudge-Toter

JIM GAGE came to Cornerstone that morning for no better reason than to get a hair-cut at Mel Crisp's barber shop. His wife insisted, and the big boss of the JG horse ranch tended to let her have her way, in some matters anyhow. He rode his no longer young, but still handsome, black stallion into town. The horse admired by all friends of Nevada Jim in Cornerstone County was left tethered close handy to a trough while his master, his dark hair greying a little at the temples nowadays, submitted to gabby Crisp's snipping, also his gossip.

The three strangers who had arrived earlier to buy supplies were now hanging around and coming under the wary scrutiny of Rick Dane, deputy to the county sheriff. Rick didn't like their looks; could anybody?

A few moments before Crisp finished brushing Jim off, the three converged on the hitch rail to inspect the big charcoal. Hank by name, the stallion was as leery of them as Deputy Dane or, for that matter, any other townmen watching.

"What d'you say, Uncle Carl?" asked the blond man with the button nose. "Figure you can tell a critter's age as good as you used to?"

"I forget nothin'." This retort was muttered by a craggy-featured six-footer, shabby, beady-eyed and gun-hung. "I only need to check his teeth. Hold still, damn you!"

He snarled the rebuke the moment he grasped at the black's muzzle. Hank was a one-man horse who could be handled by old friends of his master but not by strangers, especially the mean-tempered kind, and promptly flinched. He did more than flinch when the stranger cursed and struck at him. Loosing a nicker of indignation, he reared and, in his haste to get clear of those flailing forehooves, his assailant caught the backs of his knees against the end of the trough and flopped into it. With the splash, passers-by gave vent to their mirth.

"You shouldn't've laughed," the third stranger chided. He was bulky, a scruffy moustache completely obscuring his mouth. "Carl don't like gettin' laughed at."

Dripping water and wild-eyed with fury, the man called Carl struggled from the trough and unbuckled his pants-belt.

"I'll allow no animal to humiliate me!" he fumed.

Rick Dane would have bounded off the opposite sidewalk but, at that moment, Jim Gage emerged from Crisp's, took in the scene at a glance and reacted swiftly. Before the stallion's would-be assailant could swing the buckle, he was off the sidewalk and between them, and swinging. That mighty uppercut sent the wild one sprawling and the other strangers muttered oaths and rushed the big man.

There were many watchers, including the blacksmith Griff Tedrow and the deputy, who would have dashed to Jim's aid had they thought it necessary. But, as the blacksmith remarked to Gordy Peck, Cornerstone's undertaker and Jack-of-all-trades, "Only three of 'em. Be a cold day in hell when Jim Gage can't handle three such lowdowns."

The blond man was clinging to Jim's back but, for the moment, Jim was ignoring him; that one hadn't managed to pin his arms and the third man was squaring off to throw a punch at his face. Jim's left fist bloodied his ear, the impact started him reeling and then the man clinging to his back got his comeuppance. He yelped in pain and lost his grip; all Jim had to do was thrust a hand over his shoulder, feel for the blond head and grasp an ear — and twist it. Rid of his burden, he turned and slammed two hard ones to his ribs. Groaning, the blond man flopped to his knees.

"Stay that way," Jim growled at him, then glanced at the other two. The wild one was in a sitting posture now, spitting out a front tooth, the other prone, gasping, holding a red-smeared bandanna to his right ear. "Same goes for you two."

Sheriff Ben Courtney, showing his age but still active, approached unhurried, trading nods with his old friend. Mel Crisp said scathingly, "No man lower than a horse-beater."

"Hank okay?" Courtney asked solicitously.

"Fine, Ben," said Jim, fondling the black mane. "The wet one, the scarecrow, was about to clobber him with his belt buckle."

"That's how it was," offered Dane, who had advanced from the opposite walk. "Jim put him down fast and the other two got the fool notion they could finish what he started."

"Headed home, Jim?" prodded Courtney. Jim nodded. "Fine. Say hallo to May for me. Rick, we'll let these trailbums cool off in jail, but just till tomorrow morning." He eyed the strangers sternly. "Then you'll quit this territory, if you know what's good for you."

If looks could kill, the glare aimed at Jim by the rogue still gripping the tongue-end of his belt would have done it. Jim ignored him, turned his back and slipped the black's rein to swing astride. He had made it clear he could handle more than double his weight in hard cases. Now he had no further interest in the unkempt trio.

There was grace in his movements as he stepped up to leather. Sometimes called Nevada Jim, he was just as often referred to as Big Jim, and aptly. His six feet five inch body was muscular with no excess fat; he was a handsome veteran in well-fitting range clothes.

The man called Carl watched him ride out with hate in his heart.

"Unstrap your sidearms, rise and start walking," ordered the deputy.

After the lawmen had installed them in separate single cells, the strangers gave aliases, calling themselves Morton, Jones and Williams. Almost immediately afterward, a recently arrived citizen bustled into the sheriff's office, black-garbed and toting a Bible, his eyes gleaming with evangelical zeal. Pudgy Jarold Sims had settled in Cornerstone some eighteen months ago. The redemption of wrong-doers was his constant pre-occupation, and he worked hard at it.

"What kept you, Deacon?" asked Dane, trading winks with the sheriff. "Must be near two minutes since we locked up those miserable miscreants. You must've seen the ruckus, so how come you weren't at our heels — just like always?"

"May I visit them at once?" begged Sims. "I saw what they did. Oh, glory!

They need me so desperately, need to hear the Lord's word!"

"Sure need to change their ways," Courtney agreed. "They seem a touch more ornery than payday brawlers."

Dane let the non-conformist preacher into the jail, invited him to knock when he was ready to leave and re-secured the dealwood door.

When Sims began his spiel, Willy Stack and Noach Pacey, the occupants of the cells left and right of Carl Mulhauser's, anticipated that he would be subjected to a burst of profanity. But Mulhauser surprised them, so much so that they discreetly refrained from interjecting. With a fine show of penitence, Stack's still-damp uncle assured Sims.

"I already regret my sins, Reverend. I am sick with shame."

"You've seen the light!" enthused Sims. "The Lord be praised!"

"And, before me and my friends quit this territory, I must beg his forgiveness, the man I so offended,"

Mulhauser declared. "It was Old Nick himself possessed me. Was I out of my mind — that I should seek to inflict pain on an animal? I beg you, Reverend, tell me his name and where I can find him. I crave his forgiveness. There'll be no peace for me till he pardons me."

"Well, Jim Gage is a just and reasonable man, a gentleman," grinned Sims. "He owns the JG horse ranch northeast of town."

Guileless, easily deceived, he fell into the trap and talked incessantly for ten minutes. Mulhauser was spared the need to ask questions. Just by letting this sin-killer run off at the mouth, he learned all he wanted to know about the big man of Cornerstone County and the magnificent charcoal he had broken and trained, and named after the orneriest noncom of the regiment in which he had served long years ago, the 11th Cavalry.

Sims was out of breath when he departed. Willy Stack then demanded of his kinsman, "What was *that* all about?"

"You know me well enough to've guessed," Mulhauser said grimly. "A gentleman he's called, the giant that robbed me of a tooth and so values his devil horse." The hazy brown eyes dilated. "He has to pay! He has to suffer! All the years I was cooped in that stinkin' prison, I had to live with humiliation — and I'll take no more of it from any man nor beast!"

Pacey, a venal opportunist, had partnered up with Stack for only one reason. In played-out mining towns such as Santa Paula, Colorado, a thief could still enrich himself. Prospectors lingered, staying on to mine claims for what gold was there to be found. And Santa Paula still had a bank. He now reminded Mulhauser, "You got a bigger score to settle with a jasper name of Farwell. Gettin' sidetracked, ain't you? Why tangle with this Gage hombre?"

"He has to pay!" raged Mulhauser.

Stack signalled Pacey to guard his

tongue. Pacey, recalling his first impression of Stack's kinsman a few days before, obeyed the younger man's signal. They had been up north, waiting in sight of the gates of the Daggart Penitentiary when Mulhauser, his long term ended, emerged. At once, Pacey had realised the nephew had not exaggerated. His uncle was a shortfused powder-keg, a man obsessed with a hunger for vengeance, probably deranged. He and Stack had acquired for the ex-convict, by their own nefarious means, a saddle-animal, weapons and cash enough to provision here in Cornerstone for their long journey.

"You're the boss, Uncle Carl," Stack said placatingly. "Whatever you want us to do, we'll do it."

"Let that be understood," mumbled Mulhauser. He squatted on his bunk, seemingly oblivious to the sodden condition of his clothing. "I'm to be obeyed."

He was still playing his role of a man who had seen the error of his ways, still feigning contrition, when the three were turned loose next morning. Returning their weapons, Rick Dane told them, "Your horses and provisions are still at the barn alongside Tedrow's forge. Just saddle up and ride out, and never come back."

They rode southward out of town a little while later but, once they were clear of the outskirts, travelled a wide half-circle to make their way to the green acres of the JG ranch.

Their approach was stealthy. A cluster of boulders provided concealment for men and horses and a sweeping view of JG's whole south quarter. In the distance, horses grazed. Closer at hand, in rifle range, was an animal Mulhauser recognized. To be doubly sure, he studied the black through the spyglass passed him by Pacey.

Hank stood proud atop a low rise, his favourite spot since being put to stud, retired from active duty in deference to his advanced years.

"Too bad he ain't saddled with Gage sittin' him," leered Mulhauser, as he and his cohorts readied their rifles. "But this'll grieve the big man sore enough to please me. A horse for a tooth — the proud horse of a proud man."

"No hired hands in sight, just horses," Pacey observed as he took aim.

"But, soon as we do it, we best get movin' fast," muttered Stack.

The rifles barked. They saw the stallion lurch and begin falling, then hastily sheathed their weapons, remounted and made off, keeping the bulk of the rock cluster between them and JG range.

Three hands heard the echo of the shots and rode to investigate, one of them Dewey Hollis, a callow youth when befriended by Jim Gage years before, now in his mid-twenties and his trusted foreman. Rising in his stirrups, he called to the other riders and pointed to the low rise.

"It's Hank — and he's down!"

They heeled their mounts to a gallop and, reaching the rise, climbed to its summit. Dewey and a lean breaker named Buck Hackett dismounted. The third hand, lank-haired Pete Masseau, sat his horse and scanned the surrounding terrain.

"Aw, hell," sighed Hackett. "Looks like he took four slugs, Dewey. A great horse and strong, but he can't last."

Dewey swallowed a lump in his throat as Hackett reached to his holster.

"No, Buck," he said. "Jim ought to be here. I'll fetch him fast."

As the younger man remounted, Masseau spoke quietly. "I'll be scoutin' for tracks of the sonsabitches that did this."

The ranch-house and outbuildings were a fair distance west and out of sight and sound of the scene of the tragedy. Dewey raced his mount in that direction while the aging Dowells, fixtures at JG, shared the shade of the front porch, Ma shelling peas, her wizened spouse whittling. Jim and his wife, a good-looking woman whose neat figure hadn't deteriorated with maternity, stood in the ranch-house entrance watching their small son playing in the front yard. The scene was tranquil till Dewey was sighted, coming in at speed and yelling to a hired hand, "Saddle a horse for Jim!"

He reined up in a flurry of dust a few yards from two-and-a-half-year-old Christopher Lewis Gage, named for his father's dead brother and his mother's now-deceased Uncle Lew.

"Trouble?" called Jim.

"Hank's been shot!" Dewey shakily.

"Dear God," breathed May.

Pa Dowell swore luridly and, for once, his hefty wife did not reprimand him. Pain showed in Jim's eyes. He didn't wait to fetch his Stetson nor strap on a pistol, just bounded from the porch to the corral where one of his employees was saddling up for him. Moments later, he and Dewey were headed across the green flats at a gallop, riding stirrup to stirrup.

Reaching the rise, they dismounted quickly. Jim was tight-faced now. He squatted to lift the dying black's head onto his lap, to mutter comfortingly and stroke the gleaming neck. Hackett observed, almost choking on his words, "Plain enough he knows it's you — knows your voice — your touch."

They were staring at each other; Jim was certain Hank could see him, was recognizing him.

"He must be — hurtin' bad," mumbled Dewey.

"Time you stopped suffering old friend," Jim said gently. "Always knew this time'd come, didn't we? But we never guessed it'd have to be like this." He winced and raised his right hand. "Buck."

"Sure," nodded Hackett.

He drew and offered his six-gun. Just as Jim took it from him, just as he was about to thumb back the hammer, the black looked up at him, snorted and stopped breathing. Dewey dropped to his knees to check. His eyes were filling. Embarrassed, he turned his head away and assured Jim.

"He's gone."

The big man sighed heavily, still squatting, still with the great head resting on his lap.

"Almost — as if he read my mind," he said wistfully. "If horses could talk, I think he'd have said 'It's okay. I know you don't want to do it, so I'll make it easy for you.' That sound crazy, too sentimental?"

"Sounds just right," said Hackett, as Jim returned his gun.

Jim patted the gleaming black neck, bowed his head and muttered, "Adios, amigo."

Masseau now returned to report, "Three of 'em. I found the spent shells back there." He gestured to the rocks. "They took off southeast, ridin' like hell."

"Southeast," frowned Jim. "All right, I think I know who to look for."

"You do?" challenged Dewey.

"I tangled with 'em in town

yesterday," said Jim. "No doubt in my mind. One of 'em has a mean streak. This was his way of punishing me."

"Spite," sneered Masseau, spitting in disgust.

"When I run him to ground, he'll learn something about punishment," declared Jim. He began rising, gently lowering the dead stallion's head to the grass. "Listen now, here's where I want Hank buried. He liked this place. I won't be here, but . . . "

"He won't be left for the buzzards," promised Hackett.

"Not *this* horse," said Masseau. "I'll have some of the boys fetch spades and — we'll do it right."

"Got to get back now."

Jim took a last long look at the loyal animal, the one-man horse who had carried him into and out of countless run-ins with the scum of the frontier, as he and Dewey remounted.

While they were riding back to the ranch headquarters, Dewey began pleading.

"You got to take me along. I've sided you many a time."

"Forget it," said Jim. "You were always a reliable sidekick, no question about that, but now you're my ramrod. I have to count on you to run things while I'm gone."

"You could be gone quite a time," said Dewey.

"For as long as it takes," Jim said grimly. With the ranch-house in sight, he told Dewey, "You know which horse to saddle for me."

"Junior," nodded Dewey. "Who else? You'll be huntin' them that butchered his pa."

Before entering the house, Jim spoke briefly to the Dowells. The sympathy they felt for him wasn't expressed verbally; the old couple just looked at him. He moved into the kitchen to trade stares with his wife.

"Hank . . . ?" she began.

"They'll bury him on his lookout post," he muttered.

"Jim." She hooked her arms about

his neck. "Do I have to tell you — how I feel for you? That beautiful animal was — like family."

"Good place for him to die," he said huskily. "But not like that. I'm going after the scum who did this, honey. No guessing how long it'll take, but try to understand. It's something I have to do. I have to — get a few things. You want to pack some provisions for me?"

She made short work of that, then went to their bedroom. He had finished loading the Winchester presented to him by old cavalry buddies when he mustered out of the 11th to begin his long search for the murderer of his brother, Lieutenant Christopher Gage of that same regiment. Now he was strapping on the other gift, an ivory-butted, long-barrelled Cavalry Colt.

"You need at least one spare shirt," she murmured, moving to the dresser.

"I hope you realize it's not just because they killed Hank," he said earnestly.

"Considering how much he meant to you, and for so long, that'd be reason enough," she sighed.

"More to it than that," he told her. "May, I had a run-in with three trailtramps in town yesterday. The eldest, a wild-eyed hombre, was bumped into a trough by Hank. He was out of control, about to lash at Hank with a belt buckle."

"So you had to discourage him." May shrugged resignedly. "And, the way you fight when roused, you took care of the other two."

"I can't think of anybody else who'd work off their crazy spite the way they have," he said. "But think about it, May. Men of that low calibre are a menace, and not just to a helpless horse, so they have to be stopped. They're the kind who make widows, leave grief and misery everywhere they roam."

"I could remind you there are law officers paid to deal with such rogues," she said.

"I need no reminding," said Jim. "If, by the time I find them, they're in some cowtown jail awaiting trail, that'll be the end of it. I'll head straight for home — you have my word on that. All that matters is that they be stopped, don't you see? I have to be sure they're no danger to anybody else."

"Too bad you used to be Sergeant Gage and not just a trooper," she complained. "You've always had an over-developed sense of responsibility, and don't deny it."

"Look, I'll miss you as much as you'll miss me," he said, taking her into his arms. "But we've come a long way together, sweetheart. It's different now. You're the lady of the house and I have seven horse breakers on my payroll, tough jaspers loyal to the spread, to you and the boy, to the Dowells. I'm leaving you in safe hands. If JG were raided — and that's mighty unlikely — you and little Chris'd have all the protection you need. I wouldn't leave if I weren't certain of that."

"You fear for the safety of other people those scavengers could harm," she said kissing him. "But you might as well admit it, because it's true and I don't blame you for it, this is something you feel you owe Hank."

"True enough," he nodded. "I've never lied to you. I won't start now."

"So do what you have to do," she urged. "Look to your own protection — you veteran warrior — but keep me in mind. Wire me whenever you find a Western Union Office. You know Wes Ackroyd will get your messages to me as quickly as possible, even if he has to ride out here personally."

"I'll have ample cash for expenses," he assured her. "I'm packing everything I'm apt to need, including spare ammunition."

"Well, you won't have to take a pack-animal along," she said with a faint smile. "Because — naturally — you'll be riding Junior, Hank the Second, and he's as big and strong as his sire." She clung to him. "We'll say goodbye here and now. I don't want Dewey or Ma and Pa Dowell to see me blubbering."

Five minutes later, when the big man emerged from the house toting his gear, Ma Dowell planted a kiss on his chin; that was as high as she could reach. Pa Dowell shook his hand and muttered, "Find the polecats and let 'em have it."

Dewey stood by a young replica of the slain stallion, as coal-black, as proud of stance as his sire and as obedient to the man who had trained him. Jim slid his Winchester into the saddle-sheath. Dewey helped him secure saddlebags, packroll and provisions.

"You kept 'em in prime workin' order, the long gun and your Colt," he remarked as Jim swung astride. "Jim, I ain't bloodthirsty. I was just a sprig when you took me in hand and you taught me good. But I got to say I hope . . . "

"Sure," Jim said for his ears alone.

"It's what *I* hope for, Dewey. All three of 'em for Hank, if they make a fight of it. Hasta la vista."

Riding off his land, he glimpsed four of his men digging atop the rise and deliberately skirted that area. He swung east and, soon enough, found the tracks noted by Pete Masseau. As well as being the 11th Cavalry's champion marksman, he had been the regiment's most skilled tracker. He dismounted, the better to study the hoofprints and commit details to memory.

Memories came back to him as he began pursuing his quarry. It was inevitable he should remember taking his leave of Camp Allison long years before to begin his long hunt for his brother's killer, and his feelings at that time. History was repeating itself long after he had found and paid off Jenner, the back-shooting, brandy-swigging tinhorn. He was a man-hunter again, and the sidewinders he sought had brutally slain the best four-legged friend an ex-cavalryman could wish for.

It seemed appropriate, a kind of poetic justice, that he now rode a trusty animal sired by the killer's victim.

* * *

Carl Mulhauser, meanwhile, demanded his nephew repeat all he had learned of one Reavis Farwell. Pacey had heard the story before, but had to listen again. And, while listening, he confirmed his hunch that hate and a hunger for vengeance had twisted Mulhauser's mind.

"Took his wife and kid with him when the Trans-National outfit made him manager of their bank at Santa Paula . . . " Stack dealt it out parrot-fashion. "That Colorado town was boomin' then. Big gold strike. When the pay-veins petered out and the miners started quittin', Farwell made his bosses believe Santa Paula still needed a bank. He's stayed on because his wife died and she's buried there. He's older now and the kid, his daughter, she's full-growed and quite a looker. I was there, Uncle Carl. Saw 'em both. And law? Only law in that half-alive dump is a blubber-bellied town marshal name of Deitz."

"Farwell has to die," Mulhauser said passionately. "But he must suffer first. That's what I craved all the time I sweated in that stinkin' prison."

Pacey knew it all. With three accomplices, a young Carl Mulhauser had held up the Whitton Forks branch of the Trans-National Banking Company, a hold-up that had backfired on the perpetrators, thanks to its manager at that time. Reavis Farwell had defied the robbers by hurling a paperweight at a street window, shattering it, which was more than enough to draw local lawmen to the scene. Mulhauser's fourth man, guarding their horses out front, had rashly fired on the lawmen, thus forfeiting his life. Mulhauser's cousin, Max, Stack's father, had dashed out shooting; the bank had no rear door. He too was cut down.

Up against the lawmen, and a dozen gun-toting towners backing them, Mulhauser and his surviving accomplice were forced to surrender. He had served his full term of imprisonment; the other man had been slain while attempting a breakout.

It was at the trial that Mulhauser had begun despising Farwell and vowing vengeance. While testifying as chief witness for the prosecution Farwell had thundered condemnation on the defendant, declaring the company he represented was demanding harsh penalties as a deterrent to bank robbers. He stressed that Mulhauser had shown no compassion for the terrified clients in the bank, including a pregnant woman with a badly scared child clinging to her skirts.

Small wonder the jury, in delivering a guilty verdict, had made no recommendation for leniency. Small wonder the presiding judge had handed down such a heavy sentence.

The trio travelled five more miles

with Mulhauser still ranting. Then, gradually, he simmered down.

"Tell me more about Santa Paula," he muttered.

"I've seen purtier towns," said Stack. "It must've been built fast, just frame places, planks fallin' off walls, slag-heaps both sides, east and west. Still a few fossickers grubbin' for what little gold they can find, but most of the folks thereabouts're sodbusters. There's nothin' north of Santa Paula, but farmers're raisin' hogs and such, tryin' to raise crops too, away south."

"One bank," mused Pacey.

"And there'd have to be *some* cash in it, maybe gold too," opined Stack. "You know how farm folks are. Leery of hidin' their dinero on their land. So where else could they stash what they save? Sure, that bank safe won't be empty."

"I want to hear more about the bunch willin' to throw in with me," growled Mulhauser. "Sam Elgart got out of Daggart a half-year ahead of me.

Last thing he said was he'd be roundin' up guns, gettin' a gang together. He's done that, you say?"

"By the time we make Lockhart, in Utah, Sam'll be there waitin' for us," Stack told him. "Seven wild hombres he found. So, countin' Sam, that's eight you can rely on."

"Eleven of us," grinned Pacey. "Hell, Santa Paula'll be all ours. We just ride in and take over."

Mulhauser became emotional again. "We'll loot the bank, the stores, seize everything we need," he declared. "Then I'll burn Santa Paula, all of it. And the last thing Farwell sees before I gut-shoot him will be his precious daughter bein' dragged by a whipped horse. He must die in misery, knowin' it was *me* came back to square accounts with him!"

* * *

Nine a.m. of the following morning, two tall strangers entered Arnoldsville, the seat of Arnold County in the Utah Territory. They were uncommonly tall Texans, their names were Lawrence Valentine and Woodville Emerson, but they were better known to the frontier Press, to the law and the lawless, as Larry and Stretch, the nomadic Lone Star Trouble-Shooters forever at war with two-legged predators of every variety. Their reputation was formidable, but had been wished on them; they had never sought publicity.

In their years of drifting following their mustering out of the Confederate Cavalry, these trouble-prone wanderers had made friends and enemies. One man they called friend and remembered with respect was, like them, a living legend, a Nevada horse rancher, James Carey Gage by name. Another was Dr Vincent Beaumont, an imperious and elegant gambler from New Orleans. Doc Beaumont resented their calling him friend, for he was a cynic who claimed to loathe them for their heroism and their rough ways. The poker-addicted dude regarded them as altruists, derided their championing of the oppressed and bitterly resented having been obliged to fight side by side with them on more than one hectic occasion. It was his frequently stated wish that he would never again encounter them nor, for that matter, Nevada Jim, who he scorned as another altruist.

The Texans were not to run into Jim Gage nor Doc Beaumont in Arnoldsville, but they did spot an old and much-valued ally after loafing their mounts along only a block and a half of the main street.

They reined up a short distance from the county courthouse upon recognizing one of the prisoners being unloaded from an open wagon by a deputy sheriff and hustled up the steps to the entrance. There were four, but they were concerned only for one of them, the pudgy redman.

"Holy Hannah, it's the Chief," winced

Stretch, a gangling, tow-haired and homely drifter who, upon dismounting, would be seen to be six and a half feet tall. That was his height barefoot; booted, he appeared even taller. "Hell, runt . . . "

"Uh huh," nodded Larry of the dark thatch and brawny physique. "Slow Wolf for sure."

No other man called him 'runt'. He was in fact only three inches shorter than his towering sidekick. Also, he was the thinking half of this much-travelled duo, the planner whose instinct for strategy had helped them survive countless battles with the lawless; easy-going Stretch tended to leave all the figuring to him.

"Well, doggone it," he growled. "They got him in irons and they're shovin' him into a courthouse, so that means he's in trouble again, and maybe it ain't his fault."

"He's like us," Larry said as they pointed their mounts towards the nearest livery stable. "Never starts a ruckus, but gets into strife time and time again."

"You suppose we can help him?" asked Stretch.

"Only one way to find out," shrugged Larry. "Townfolk ain't crowdin' into the courthouse, so there'll be plenty room for us. And we won't know if we can help him till we find out how he got himself arrested."

Cathcart P. Slow Wolf was a rare soul in many respects, the only son of an inept Sioux warrior and a white schoolteacher. He had inherited none of his mother's looks; nobody would doubt he was a full-blood and, indeed, his father had schooled him in Indian lore and all the redskins' skills as trackers and hunters. However, he had also learned much from his mother. She had taught him English, her favourite subject, so it had to be correct English, the language of scholars of superior education.

This was Slow Wolf's close-guarded secret. Unless in the presence of men he knew and trusted, he resorted to the broken English of 'dumb Injuns'. To show off his command of the language in earshot of rough-speaking semi-illiterates, who proliferated in 19th century frontier America, was less than wise, he had learned; poorly educated palefaces tended to violently resent a pudgy Indian who could express himself in as precise English as a college professor.

When Circuit Judge Clarence Bush took his place on the bench, Slow Wolf decided there was nothing he could do for himself but plead not guilty, tell nothing but the truth and hope the white man's justice would prevail.

He was unaware two tall friends of his were seated in the back row.

Acting as prosecutor, since none of the prisoners had committed capital offences, Sheriff Elmo Nagel began naming the defendants and listing charges.

2

Together Again

"HERMAN ROGEL and Daniel Monahan, drunk and disorderly, Your Honor," the sheriff intoned. "Whitney Pincus, felonious drilling of a hole in the wall of the Carmody residence . . . "

"Drunk and disorderly — a common offence," interjected the judge. "But I'd take it kindly, Sheriff Nagel, if you'd be a mite more specific about the offender who — drilled a hole . . . ?"

"Bathroom wall," explained Nagel. "John Carmody, a merchant of Arnoldsville, has six daughters, all full-grown, all pretty. Pincus is a Peeping Tom."

"That makes it a whole lot clearer," drawled Judge Bush.

Already, the drifters were hopeful.

How could they be wrong about Judge Bush's accent? He had to be Texan-born.

"The charge against the Indian, Slow Wolf, is the theft of a dun horse and saddle and a Winchester rifle," announced Nagel. "One of my deputies, Jay Walden, found him in possession of same and — uh — took him into custody."

"Is there an Indian Agent hereabouts?" asked Bush. "That's the question I have to raise whenever an Indian appears in my court."

"Not for a couple of hundred miles, Your Honor," said Nagel.

"You, Slow Wolf . . ." Bush addressed the redskin. "Do you understand enough English to — uh — savvy the charge?"

"Me savvy, Judge," nodded Slow Wolf.

"How about legal representation for these prisoners?" demanded Bush.

Orson Stream, a local lawyer, indicated he would be defending only one prisoner, the shifty-eyed, lip-licking Pincus. Rogel and Monahan pleaded guilty, were fined $20 and warned to moderate their intake of hard liquor and their tendency to become rowdy under the influence of same, though Bush anticipated he would be repeating his words when next he presided in Arnoldsville.

Stream made a half-hearted appeal for his client while Bush and the sheriff traded sceptical looks. Whitney Pincus, they were asked to believe, was a lover of all things beautiful including he female form. As he was a bachelor and as Arnoldsville had no art gallery, he was reduced to the ignominy of surreptitious surveillance of the community's more attractive female citizens. Bush dismissed the defence appeal as being typical of what people try to avoid stepping into while crossing cowpastures, sentenced the defendant to thirty days in the county jail and daily duty as a cleaner of the latrines in the jailhouse yard. He also ordered the confiscation of Pincus' equipment; whatever tools he used for drilling holes in bathroom walls.

Having disposed of Rogel, Monahan and the peeper, he questioned the swarthy half-breed again. As Slow Wolf had no legal representation and was waiving his right to a jury hearing, was he willing to testify in his defence under oath, and did he understand the oath?

"Swear on Bible — to great White Spirit — to speak straight," nodded Slow Wolf. "Me savvy."

"Take the stand," ordered Bush. "Sheriff, administer the oath."

During this, Bush scrutinized the accused. Slow Wolf was bulky and self-effacing, clad in fringed buckskin and moccasins, his moon-face crowned by jet-black hair, braids of it dangling to his shoulders. He held his headgear on his lap, a beaver hat with a turkey feather sticking up from the band at the rear.

"As Deputy Walden was the arresting officer . . . " began Nagel.

"He may question the prisoner," nodded Bush.

Walden, a surly-looking character, confronted Slow Wolf and urged him confess all, reminding him he was under oath.

"No-account Injun like you, a loner, could get himself a good horse and a fine Winchester only one way," he growled. "Where'd you steal 'em?" He remarked to the judge before Slow Wolf could answer.

"You find a driftin' Injun, you just *know* he didn't pay for the horse he's ridin' nor anything he's totin'."

"All lone Indians are thieves — that's the prosecution case?" frowned Bush. "Well now, let's hear the defendant's side of it."

"Me no steal," mumbled Slow Wolf. "Horse, saddle and long gun mine."

"You claimin' you bought 'em?" jeered Walden. "C'mon, show us a bill of sale."

"Presents," Slow Wolf said doggedly. "White men buy um for me."

"Who does he think he's foolin'?" Walden appealed to Bush.

"How long ago was this?" asked Bush.

"Many moons," said the defendant.

"It'd help your case if you could at least remember the names of those white men," Bush told him.

"Good friends," said Slow Wolf. "Valentine, Emerson. Friend Lawrence, friend Woodville."

"How can he prove that?" challenged Walden.

"So now we have a problem, and it's a jim-dandy," declared Bush. "Being Texan myself, I've followed the career of those outlaw-fighters with more than a little interest. But the problem is they could be anywhere between the Missouri and California at this time."

Only fifteen or so locals were in attendance for want of something better to do. They'd been bored by the proceedings until the Texans got to their feet and Larry called, "We're right here, Judge."

"Darned if you aren't," grinned Bush.

"Just got in," offered Stretch.

"Approach the bench, gentlemen," ordered Bush.

"Gentlemen?" protested Walden. "What kind of white men'd side with a lousy Injun?"

"Sheriff Nagel, I suggest . . . " began Bush.

"Right, Your Honor," nodded Nagel. "Jay, button your lip."

The tall men ambled down the centre aisle to be recognized with deep gratitude by the defendant.

"Good friends," he said fervently.

"Nice seein' you again, ol' buddy," drawled Larry.

"How you been, Chief?" grinned Stretch.

"Not happy in paleface calaboose," replied Slow Wolf. "Feel better now."

"Well now, this is something," Bush eyed the drifters amiably. "Couple good ol' boys from the Lone Star. You can support the accused's claim?"

"Be right proud to, Judge," said Stretch. "But — uh — better my partner does the palaverin'. He always talks for us."

"The prisoner can step down," said Bush. "Take the stand, Mister Valentine. Sheriff, swear him in." When this was done, he enquired of the witness, "Just what can you tell us?"

"Slow Wolf don't lie," shrugged Larry. "It was us fixed him up with a dun pony and a saddle, the Winchester too. Kind of a partin' gift, you know? Only we've met up with him a time or two since back then."

"I'm still interested," prodded Bush. "You gonna vouch for his good character?"

"Be glad to," nodded Larry. "The thing about Slow Wolf is he's — well — a different kind of Injun. Never was a warrior, never ever lifted a scalp. He just hunts and drifts. Claims he's a coward, and that's kind of a joke."

"Why so?" demanded Bush.

"We saved his hide, but he's saved ours," declared Larry. "When the chips're down, he'll handle his share of fightin'. He don't enjoy it none, but he does it."

"Injun-lover!" accused Walden.

"Silence!" Bush rapped with his gavel. "One more yap out of you, Deputy, and I fine you for contempt of court. And I don't mean nickels and dimes, hear? A *heavy* fine. Take you a month of Sundays to pay it off."

Seated with head bowed, Slow Wolf hoped his sighs of relief were inaudible. Not only were his loyal Texan friends saving his bacon; by showing up right now, they had spared him the need to break his secret. This wasn't his first time in court. On previous occasions he'd had no option but to demonstrate his impressive command of the white man's language. And how he hated the startled stares of judges, attorney and lawmen, not to mention the indignation of half-educated onlookers.

Bush delivered his verdict. The word

of a fellow-Texan was good enough for him. He found the defendant not guilty, ordered him released from custody and his property returned.

The tall men tagged along when Sheriff Nagel, after freeing Slow Wolf of his manacles, took him back to his office to collect his personal effects. Discreetly, the three compadres postponed conversation until they were out of earshot of the county jail and headed for the barn at which the pudgy half-breed's dun was stabled.

"That deputy bein' a mean hombre, you hanker to vamoose," guessed Larry.

"Muy pronto." Stretch added his guess.

"The injustice of it," grouched Slow Wolf. "Deputy Walden is a bigot, a curmudgeon with no more imagination than a mule."

"He's an Injun-hater," shrugged Stretch. "To a sorehead like him, one Injun's no better'n another."

"I believe it would be beneficial to

my welfare to make a speedy departure from Arnold County," muttered Slow Wolf.

"Well, look, we only stopped by to pick up a few necessaries, tobacco, whiskey and such," said Larry. "That won't take long, so how about you stay close to us and we'll ride out together?"

They were gone from Arnoldsville some thirty minutes later, Larry, Stretch and their half-Sioux crony, a mixed trio straddling a sorrel, a pinto and a dun respectively, not hustling, letting their mounts amble eastward.

"Utah's all right," Stretch remarked. "But, this time of year, the huntin's good in Colorado, the fishin' too."

"That's where we're headed, ol' buddy, and you're invited," offered Larry.

Slow Wolf winced uneasily.

"Forgive my apprehension, dear friends of mine. It always gladdens my heart, meeting you again. However, on every other such occasion keeping you company has been detrimental to my nerves and, indeed, my personal welfare."

"Whatsamatter?" challenged Stretch. "You afeared we'll ride into some kind of ruckus?"

"Don't you always?" frowned Slow Wolf.

"Hey, we don't get into a scrap every damn week of the year," cajoled Larry.

"I bet we can make it from here to the Rockies peaceable," Stretch said bravely. "Any towns we find, we'll just provision up and keep movin'."

"Maybe bunk overnight in a hotel if we got a mind to," said Larry. "But just that long. Overnight. No lingerin' to mix into no hassles."

"I don't doubt your good intentions," sighed Slow Wolf. "But, as reasonable men, you must admit . . . "

"Well, yeah, we tangle with a lot of town rowdies and owlhooters and badge-toters," Larry conceded. "But that's mostly accidental."

"Tell you what, Chief," suggested Stretch. "First time it looks like we're gonna be in trouble, you can skedaddle. We won't blame you, and no hard feelin's."

"It's just that, as I've so often assured you, I'm allergic to fisticuffs and gunfights," declared Slow Wolf. "I am a devout coward dedicated to my own welfare."

"Fine by us," shrugged Larry. "So what d'you say?"

"Your agreeable companionship would be most welcome," said Slow Wolf. "I accept your invitation on the clear understanding that . . . "

"Whatever you say," Stretch drawled comfortingly. "Soon as somethin' makes you nervous, you get lost."

"Now we got that settled, how've you been since last time our trails crossed?" asked Larry.

"Please don't take offence," said Slow Wolf. "But life is quiet and uneventful for me — *until* our trails cross."

* * *

Jim Gage was a patient man, maybe more so than two Texans he now and then remembered. The storm he rode into obliterated tracks of his quarry, a wailing wind raising great dust clouds, sweeping all hoofprints away, but he didn't let his temper flare. It seemed more reasonable to give thanks for finding his way to a regular trail and, an hour later, glimpsing a Wells Fargo relay station ahead.

The storm lasted ten hours during which he sheltered with the family running the way station, grateful for their hospitality and a roof over his head. Hank Junior was comfortable, taking his ease in a stall of the weatherproof barn. No member of the family had sighted three riders in this area before the storm hit. That, he decided, was too much to hope for.

When the storm broke and he was ready to resume his search, he was told the next town east on the stage route was Lydell City, Utah Territory. He would cross the border within an hour and could expect to make the seat of Lydell County around noon of the morrow.

So Lydell City was to be his next destination; bound to be a Western Union Office there, and it was high time he wired May a reassuring message.

West and east of the Utah border, while en route to Lydell City, he quit the stage trail at intervals to hunt for a sign of the horse-shooters. No luck, but he wasn't about to give up. The pain was still in him, the grim indignation, the sense of loss, the determination to face the crazed man with the wild eyes and thin-lipped mouth. The others too, all three of them.

As the people at the Wells Fargo station had predicted, he reached Lydell City, a sizeable trail town, in the heat and glaring sunlight of the noon hour. A livery stable was his first stop.

The hostler, a connoisseur from way back, ran an admiring eye over the black as Jim led him in.

"Feed, rubdown, the best of everything," Jim instructed him.

"Mister, only the best care'd be good enough for him," enthused the stablehand. "You sure savvy horses."

"Had some experience," said Jim with a wry grin.

"Needs special handlin', huh?"

"He appreciates good care, won't give you any trouble. Only thing you have to remember, in case you crave the pleasure of straddling him, is he's a one-man horse."

"Won't let no other man mount him?"

"Well, I'll put it this way. Any other man wouldn't stay on him long."

"Thanks for the advice. I'll treat him good."

Jim found the telegraph office and got off a brief but sufficient message to May. He was in good health, still searching, and she need not be worried about him.

He should pick up a few extra

provisions here, he decided, but first lunch. A diner or a saloon? The latter appealed most; a not too noisy saloon providing a varied counter-lunch and cold beer.

Soon afterward, in one of Lydell City's better bars, he traded friendly talk with the dispenser of cheer, built a couple of thick sandwiches of ham, pickles and sliced hardboiled eggs. These and a tankard of beer were all he needed right now. He didn't feel like eating on his feet so, when a couple of dapper customers, obviously drummers, began vacating a corner table, he carried his lunch over there.

"Finished with that?" he asked, as one of the men dropped a folded newspaper on the table.

"All yours, friend."

The drummers departed. Jim made himself comfortable, began satisfying his appetite and thirst and unfolded the newspaper. It had been published quite a distance from here, the Whitton Forks *Dispatch*. He had heard of Whitton

Forks, a town up by the Nevada-Oregon border. The front page story was of little interest to him. He read some of it, then turned the page and did get interested.

The face in the photograph stared out at him from under the heading of a full column report, the release from the Daggart Penitentiary of one Carl Mulhauser. Recognition was immediate. How could he forget that face, the fearsome visage of a sadistic rogue who, but for his swift intervention, would have stuck old Hank with the buckle end of a belt? So now he had a name to match the face.

He finished eating, drained his tankard and signalled the barkeep, who obliged by fetching a refill. Then he read and absorbed the report of the crime for which the wild-eyed one had served a long prison term, a bank robbery thwarted by the bank's plucky manager, the Whitton Forks lawmen and more than a few fired-up locals. So the bank manager, Reavis Farwell, was chief prosecution witness and quite an orator, a real spellbinder according to the writer of this story.

"Mulhauser, you have a fixation," he reflected. "That's the word — fixation — a craze to avenge yourself. I'm getting to understand the way your mind works."

With only two sidekicks, Mulhauser had to deny himself the savage pleasure of raiding the well-manned headquarters of the JG spread in hopes of paying off its owner for putting him down with one hard blow. Somehow, he must have learned of the strong bond between the JG boss and the old but still proud black stallion. Somebody had shot off his mouth. Who? His friends Ben Courtney and Rick Dane were men of discretion. He could think of none of his Cornerstone cronies who would visit three such unprepossessing strangers in the county jail. One possibility, he decided. Sims, the preacher, the would-be reformer bent on saving souls, was a regular visitor whose timing was deplorable. Saturday night drunks plagued by hangovers had actually complained to the sheriff that Sim's babbled sermons only increased their misery.

And Sims was a gossip-monger, which explained how Mulhauser and his hangers-on had found their way to JG range — and the defenceless Hank — after Courtney had turned them loose.

"I was right about you," Jim muttered softly, studying the evil face again. "To your twisted way of thinking, shooting Hank was a means of punishing me."

In his disgust, his first impulse was to crumple the newspaper and toss it aside. But he resisted that urge, finished his beer and rolled and lit a cigarette. Then he detached page 3, folded both sides of the column and carefully tore it out. The picture — how could he have contemplated discarding it? Worth a thousand words. People questioned during his hunt might be confused by a verbal description, but not by the photograph. That face. Once seen, never forgotten.

He folded the strip with care, stowed it in his wallet and got to his feet. After paying and tipping the barkeep, he moved out into the sunlight.

He wondered if the local law would prove a source of information. Well, a courtesy call on the sheriff could do no harm. He took an after-lunch stroll and found his way to Lydell City's administration building. It had two entrances, one opening onto a flight of stairs leading up to the mayor's office and a meeting room, the other giving access to the office of County Sheriff B. W. Tyrell with the county jail at the rear.

He knocked, entered and apologized for interupting the sheriff's lunch. Tyrell, a heavyset, short-bearded man, was seated behind his desk, eating with a napkin tucked into his collar.

"Doesn't have to be an interruption at all, Sheriff," he suggested. "You can keep eating while we talk. Gage is the name, James C. Gage."

"Got no objection to conversation with a meal," shrugged Tyrell. "Make yourself comfortable. Gage? Name's familiar. Horse rancher from up by the Humboldt River territory, and some call you Nevada Jim?"

"Well, we breed and train good stock at JG," said Jim. "My customers come from all over."

"You're *that* Gage," nodded Tyrell. "Thoroughbreds, quarter horses, team animals, you supply all kinds." He munched and swallowed. "So, something I can do for you?"

"That depends on whether or not the men I'm looking for passed through here," said Jim. "I can name one of 'em now, and I have his picture."

"What's the name?" asked Tyrell.

"Carl Mulhauser," said Jim, digging out his wallet. "Released from the Daggart prison less than a month ago."

Tyrell inspected the strip of newsprint, concentrating mostly on the photograph.

He grimaced as he returned it.

"Like the face of the devil himself."

"More devil than saint, to put it mildly," Jim assured him.

"He can't have been in my bailiwick," declared Tyrell. "That's a face I'd remember, believe me."

"How about your deputies?" asked Jim.

"If either of 'em had spotted that heller, I'd know," said Tyrell. "A mean one like that Mulhauser, bet your life Rorke or Mershey would tip me off rightaway. Sorry, Gage. No chance they showed 'emselves around here."

"I tagged their tracks southeast till a wind storm blew them away," frowned Jim. "It's possible they're riding around towns this size. When they need to reprovision, Mulhauser might send one of his companeros in. He probably knows the Whitton Forks paper reported his release and printed his picture."

"Want to tell me why you're huntin' 'em?" prodded Tyrell.

"They killed an old friend of mine," said Jim.

"Well, hell!" exclaimed Tyrell. "If there's a murder warrant circulating, I'd have a copy in my files, and I don't!"

"The law wouldn't call it murder," Jim said bitterly. "My friend was four-legged, Sheriff. Best horse I ever owned. He was well on in years. I'd put him to stud. One he sired — dead ringer for him — is the horse I'm using now."

Tyrell nodded thoughtfully.

"Man's apt to get used to one special horse if it's served him well," he remarked. "I know the feeling. There was an appaloosa I owned when I was a helluva lot younger. Finally died of old age. Damned if I don't still mourn him." He eyed him intently. "How'd it happen?"

"Some of my hands heard the shooting, but from a distance," said Jim. "Rifle-fire. Sounded like all three of 'em cut loose at the same time. Four bullets hit Hank."

"Am I reading your mind?" Tyrell chose his words with care. "I figure you for a responsible kind of man, Gage, a clear thinker. Wouldn't take the law into your own hands, would you?"

"No," said Jim. "But somebody has to run 'em to ground. They do have to be stopped."

"Because they got to be bad medicine," agreed Tyrell. "Any hard cases who'd kill a horse that way, they just couldn't be law-abiding."

"I don't believe they're looking for honest work," Jim said scathingly. He rose to leave. "Hope I didn't spoil your appetite."

Tyrell sipped coffee and shook his head.

"No. But where do you go from here?"

"I'll provision up and scout some more," decided Jim. "The territory southeast of here I guess. I'll know their tracks when I cut 'em again."

"I sure wish you luck," muttered

Tyrell. "You know I mean that, Gage."

"Sure," nodded Jim.

From the sheriff's office, he headed for a general store, made a few purchases there and started for the livery stable. The store clerk had parcelled his purchases. The parcel was tucked under an arm and he was moving slowly, deep in thought. A clue was his greatest need right now, a hunch, some indication of the ultimate destination of Mulhauser and his cronies. After serving his time, a jailbird has to go *somewhere*. He resolved to re-read the newspaper report, but later, when he was night-camped a good distance to the southeast.

Now came a distraction, the kind of coincidence so often experienced by two wanderers he had never forgotten. He was passing a saloon when an unwanted patron was unceremoniously expelled. Propelled by the bouncer's hard kick, a small, buck-toothed Mexican came hurtling out to flop in the dust. A battered guitar had been smashed over his head, the wreckage of it adhering to his neck and shoulders. The bouncer emerged scowling and flung a sweat-stained sombrero at him.

"And never show your greaser face in here again!" he snarled. A lawman was approaching, a stockily-built defender of the peace with a bulbous nose and bags under his eyes. The bouncer growled at him while Jim surveyed the whining little man floundering in the dust, the last man he wished to encounter here in Lydell City or, for that matter, anywhere else. "Kick him into a cell for panhandlin' Rorke!"

"Got your boss good and mad, did he?" asked the deputy.

"The nerve of the little polecat!" fumed the bouncer. "Can you believe he took a shine to Molly, tried to sweet-talk her? Damn him, she's been the boss's wife five years or more!"

"Maybe he thinks he's a ladies' man," Deputy Rorke said derisively, "though I'll never savvy why." The bouncer went back inside. Rorke bent, grasped the little man by an arm and hauled him upright, then put a disapproving eye on the animal tethered to the saloon hitch rail. "If that sad-lookin' roan's yours, untie it and fetch it along. It'll be kept in the jail-yard while you're sweatin' out your ten days for vagrancy."

Only now did the dusty and dishevelled Benito Espina sight the big man watching. He heaved a sigh of relief and bared his buckteeth in a gleeful leer.

"Amigo Jim! My heart sings! Ai chihuahua! This is lucky for me, no? You will help me?"

"What I ought to do, cucaracha, is finish what the bouncer started," scowled Jim. "Kick you from one end of the street to the other."

"Hey, he called you amigo," blinked Rorke.

"Don't hold it against me, Deputy," sighed Jim, producing his wallet. "The charge'll be vagrancy?" Rorke nodded, then gawked incredulously. Jim had folded a $10 bill and tucked it into a pocket of Benito's chaleco. "You saw what I did. Now he's got money in his pocket — enough to keep him out of jail?"

"Guess so," frowned Rorke, as Benito rid himself of the remains of his guitar and retrieved his sombrero. "But don't leave it at that, big feller. You got to explain, else I'll go loco tryin' to figure it out. Why'd a gent like you want to help this weasel?"

"If I told you, you'd call me a liar," Jim complained. "And suddenly you and I wouldn't be so friendly."

"I won't call you a liar," promised Rorke.

"All right," shrugged Jim. "Longer ago than I want to remember, he saved my life."

The deputy took one pace backward and loosed a gasp.

"*Him? Your* life?"

"See what I mean?" challenged Jim. "You're ready to call me a liar."

"Said I wouldn't and I won't," Rorke assured him."But you got to tell me *how*! Gimme a break! Help me understand what you're sayin'!"

The runty Mex was grinning triumphantly and untying the roan. Jim was irritated, but not by Rorke, who couldn't be blamed for his curiosity.

"All right," he said resignedly. "You ever been bitten by a rattler?"

"I'm leery of rattlesnakes." Rorke shook his head. "I've been lucky."

"Congratulations," said Jim. "There was a time *I* wasn't lucky at all. Here's where I was bitten." He indicated the small of his back. "Now ask yourself — how do you reach a wound back there, put a knife to it, get all the poison out, if you're all by yourself in the middle of nowhere?"

"Mister, you were a goner," muttered Rorke.

"Would've been, but for the Mex," Jim assured him. "He happened on me pretty soon afterward and got the job done. If he hadn't, I wouldn't be here talking to you now, telling you about it."

"Sounds wild, but I believe you," decided Rorke, before moving away. "I don't reckon you'd say it if it wasn't true."

"Ah, you do not forget, amigo," Benito said happily. "Is good we meet again, no?"

"No," growled Jim. "And stay downwind of me. Hell's sakes, when's the last time you took a bath?"

"Where we go from here?" demanded Benito.

"We?" Jim glowered at him. "Forget it. I bore having you tag me around too many years. It won't happen again, savvy? Wherever I'm going I don't want you riding in my shadow, slowing me down."

"But we are old amigos," Benito protested. "I save your life. Is like we are hermanos."

"I settled my debt to you years ago, and more than once," retorted Jim. "Saved your no-good hide time and time again, and now I've had my bellyful of rescuing you from lynch parties and husbands and shotgun-toting fathers of women you were dumb enough to woo. You're always a thorn in my side and more trouble than you're worth." He pointed warningly. "This is adios, not hasta la vista."

"My heart is sad," sighed Benito.

"Better sad heart than a sore butt," warned Jim. "When I ride out of this town, you head elsewhere or, so help me, I'll do some ass-kicking you'll never forget."

He turned his back and strode on to the livery stable, there to pay the hostler, pack his saddle-bags and ready Junior for riding. An hour later, he was gone from Lydell County and scouting the terrain southeast.

He finally found the horse tracks now so familiar, but in the hour before sundown. Now he had no option but to make his nightcamp by a creek, a tributary of the Sevier River.

3

Dude On A Bay Colt

THE creek flowed easily, the black grazed contentedly and, in the dark of early evening, the big man hunkered by his fire, waited for his supper to cook and caught up on some deep thinking.

At first, he thought of home, of May and their son, the Dowells, Dewey, the whole JG crew. The spread would function well during his absence; he hired only reliable men. Then he re-read the report of Mulhauser's release and pondered a journalist's rehashing of the Mulhauser trial.

'Prison didn't change him, didn't kill his hunger for revenge,' he mused. 'The bank manager maybe — Farwell? His testimony damned Mulhauser. Chances are he cursed Farwell every day of every year he was in Daggart, but would he go back to Whitton Forks to avenge himself against Farwell, a town that remembers him? Wait a minute. That was a long time back. Would Farwell still be there? None of us grow any younger. Farwell may have died years ago.'

So where, just where was Mulhauser bound, and for what purpose? Was he seeking a permanent refuge, a haven? That didn't seem likely. He was well-armed, as were the younger men accompanying him — hard cases for sure, trail trash. Wherever those three were headed, it had to mean trouble for somebody. He, the hunter, didn't know that somebody, but already he felt a responsibility for his — or her — welfare. If Mulhauser and his cohorts had been sighted by JG hands while lining their rifles on Hank, there would certainly have been a shootout. And, with firearms, JG hands were no greenhorns. Their gun-savvy matched their expertise at catching and breaking wild horses. The three rogues would have been the losers and no longer a menace — to anybody.

His supper was almost ready for dishing up when the slight sound alerted him, the subdued nicker of a horse, not Junior, another animal somewhere back of his camp. As he moved clear of the fireglow, he filled his hand. The long-barrelled, ivory-butted Colt cleared its greased holster smoothly and swiftly. He positioned himself behind a tree, cocked his pistol and his ears and waited and watched.

The horseman had dismounted; he sensed that. A few more minutes and he was hearing hesitant footsteps as well as the horse's plodding. Junior whinnied a greeting. His owner wasn't feeling that sociable.

As soon as he glimpsed the blurred outlines of the figure, he drew a bead and called his challenge.

"You're covered, snooper! Keep coming — with your hands up! If I see a gun, you're buzzard-bait!"

"Amigo Jim — my heart sings again!" He grimaced to the sound of the irritatingly familiar voice "Big surprise! We meet twice in the same day!" Benito came into clear view, leading the roan. "On the grave of my madre, I swear I do not follow up. Is just a happy accident I find you again."

"The hell it is, cucaracha," scowled Jim, lowering the hammer, reholstering his six-gun. "No accident. You've been tagging me since I quit Lydell City."

"Is not true." The runty Mex denied the accusation. "I am lost and hungry. I see a fire. I smell cooking. I say 'Benito, you must beg for food or you will starve.' So I come to this place and, with much joy, I find my good amigo!"

Jim contemplated him grimly. How well he knew this half-pint, this pocket-picking would-be womanizer who had clung to him like a leech during his long hunt for his brother's killer, and how he resented that, of all people, of all frontier types, it had to be Benito Espina who had saved his life. Benito bared his teeth in a cheerful grin. Jim bared his, growled ferociously and, in a quick movement, seized him.

"You're overdue for this," he declared.

And Benito loosed a wail as the big man lifted him and toted him to the creek bank.

"No — por favor! I will drown!"

Jim heaved. The little man wailed again, was temporarily airborne, then hit the stream with a splash and submerged. He surfaced, spluttering, his arms flailing.

"Don't climb out till I tell you," ordered Jim.

"Asistir!" begged Benito.

"I make it four feet deep out there," said Jim. "Only way you'll drown — and you'd be no loss — is if you keep your stinking head under, and you aren't apt to do that."

"You are cruel!"

"I'm practical. If I have to feed you, okay. But not if I have to smell you."

Jim emptied another can of beans into his skillet and put extra wood on the fire. He also unhitched his lariat and improvised a clothesline. Next he off-saddled the roan, put it to graze beside Junior and, from the packroll, unearthed the little man's blanket. Only then did he permit Benito to quit the creek, ordering him to strip, wring out and hang his duds.

A short time later, they were side by side and eating, Benito shrouded in his blanket and still complaining. His sodden garments were draped over the line, steam rising from them. This was no way, he protested, for an old friend to treat an old friend. Now he would die of pneumonia. Jim sourly replied he couldn't hope to be so lucky. Benito ate hungrily and, after a while, his gaze strayed. In the glow of the fire, Junior's hide gleamed. He and the roan were nuzzling each other.

"Your find black caballo," the little man observed. "Muy bello — and looking even younger."

Jim's face clouded over.

"That's not Hank. I call him Junior. Hank was his sire."

"Hank — he must be of a great age now," Benito remarked. "But still muy bello, si?"

"Muerto," Jim said bitterly.

"Muerto?" frowned Benito. "Amigo Jim — is a tragedia — so hermoso a caballo. I grieve for you. I will miss him."

"Sure," nodded Jim. "You really admired him. As I recall, after you drew out the poison and saved my life, I was weak for a while, couldn't stop you. You admired Hank so much you tried to steal him."

"I was ashamed," Benito said contritely.

"And sore," jibed Jim. "I calculate he bucked and threw you a couple of seconds after you mounted him."

"This one . . . ?" prodded Benito.

"Don't get the same dumb idea about Junior," warned Jim. "I trained him like I trained his pa. He's mine, a one-man horse. Insurance, if you savvy what that means. One way I can be confident no son of a bitch'll steal him."

"It has been many years," reflected Benito. "Hank was of a great age."

"He wasn't given his chance to die of old age," scowled Jim. "Three hombres cut him down with rifle-fire."

The little man was outraged.

"Bastardos! You are hunting them? I will ride with you. And, when we find them . . . !"

"This is me you're talking to, cucaracha, not some stranger," Jim reminded him. "When we find 'em, when the chips're down, you'll spook and run for cover. That's your style."

"I will stand by you," insisted Benito.

"As sure as snow falls in hell," muttered Jim.

Benito had cleaned his plate. He sipped coffee and made his pitch.

"It would be like before, my amigo. For so far, for so long, we sought the bad hombre who killed your brother. Was I not lucky for you?"

"Scarce ever," said Jim.

"I am a lonely caballero."

"Caballero? If you're a caballero, I'm a fullblood Shoshone."

"I have no place else to go, amigo. Por favor, let me ride with you, help you find these bad hombres."

Jim eyed him sidelong, realizing full well that, wherever he sought his quarry, this dissolute little Mex would tag along. If he were rejected now, he would still follow, holding back, sometimes invisible, but reappearing like magic every time he caught the aroma of cooking.

"You'll be no help," he growled.

"On the grave of my madre, I promise I will be muy bravo," grinned Benito. "I will risk my life for you."

"Some hopes," scoffed Jim. "Now *believe* this. First time I feel your thieving paws reaching for my wallet, my watch, anything that's mine, you're all through. I'll dump you in the first jail I find."

"We are together again!" Benito said elatedly. "My heart is full of . . . !"

"Yeah, you're full of it," jibed Jim. "That's for sure."

* * *

Some distance to the east, toward noon of the following day, a lone rider travelled a trail that would take him out of the Utah Territory and into the state of Colorado and, eventually, his destination.

Vincent Beaumont, physician and surgeon, a brilliant healer, was an inveterate gambler. He preferred poker to the practice of medicine, so much so that his small black valise containing his medical gear was kept out of sight in his packroll. His skill as a surgeon was formidable, but he scorned it. Any traveller passing him on this trail would have assumed him to be exactly what he claimed to be, a sporting man.

He looked the part. His headgear was a flatcrowned black Stetson with a silver band. A duster protected his custom-tailored frockcoat, striped grey pants, colorful vest and cravat and snow-white shirt. He was a handsome six-footer with a well-tended moustache. New Orleans born, he had inherited his Irish mother's temper and his aristocratic father's imperious demeanor and love of the finer things of life. He despised slovenliness and uncouth people and all men of heroic instincts, two certain Texans in particular. It was his proud claim that he was a confirmed cynic.

The sporting men's grapevine was as reliable as Western Union. Having learned of the presence of three professional gamblers, high rollers of some reputation, in the township of Sawyerville, Colorado, he was eager to join them as quickly as possible. His bankroll was healthy; it would be his pleasure to match wits and skill with other pros at a green baize table and relieve them of a fat piece of their wealth.

At this time, however, he was a mite short on provisions and feeling more than a little hungry. Sighting smoke rising from the chimney of a homestead away north of the trail, he slowed his handsome bay colt to a walk and gave some thought to detouring.

Homesteaders, farm folk probably, poorly educated, if at all. Could he endure an hour of such company? Not his kind by any means. It would be an ordeal. Still, he would adhere to his standards, the standard of a high-born gentleman. He would insist on paying for his meal, and handsomely. Also he would accord these yokels the courtesy they probably did not warrant — which would no doubt confuse the hell out of them; in a fine hotel or a homesteader's kitchen, his manners would be as impeccable as always.

He wheeled the bay off the trail and started north for the homestead, noting as he drew closer the barn and corral, the plowed fields, the chickens and hogs, a milk-cow or two. Caesar's ghost, what a dump. But, as long as the food was edible . . .

The homesteader emerged from the house to follow the horseman's approach, as did his skinny wife, his lanky tousle-haired son and skinny teenage daughter. After those four, another put in an appearance. She was of an age with the lanky young man and, to Doc's disapproving eye, extremely pregnant, a bovine female whose expression was as uncomprehending as the lanky young man's.

'Lord, give me strength,' Doc secretly prayed. 'And don't let that woman suffer contractions till long after I've eaten and departed.'

He rode into the front yard, reined up and doffed his hat.

"My name is Beaumont," he announced.

The homesteader traded glances with his wife and mumbled his response.

"Well — uh — we're the Cobbs.

This here's my wife, our little girl Viola, our boy Jesse and his wife Dora Sue. She's gonna have a baby."

'Did this peasant think I needed to be told that?' Doc wondered in exasperation.

"Company, Pa!" Son Jesse seemed overcome. "Well, shucks, we never got no visitors, not from Sawyerville, not from no place."

"Sawyerville is my destination," Doc informed him.

"You're headed right," offered Cobb. "Stay on that trail and the border's ten mile yonder. Then there's a crossroads and you swing south to Sawyerville."

"Thank you, Mister Cobb, I was already aware of that."

"Company," Jesse dazedly repeated.

"Company," echoed his wife.

"I need to rest my horse and would be obliged to join you for lunch," said Doc, producing his well-filled wallet. "As I'm an unexpected guest, I acknowledge Mrs Cobb would have to set an extra place. I trust this will recompense you?"

He proffered a $10 bill. Cobb took it from him and gawked at it. The other crowded close, squinting, obviously impressed.

"My land, will you look at that," exclaimed Ma Cobb.

"Ten dollars cash money, by damn!" gasped the homesteader. "Mister Beaumont, sir, I call this plumb generous. We're just folks and it's plain you're a genuine gentleman but, if you can abide the likes of us, I guarantee all the hospitality we can give you."

"A meal and care of my horse will suffice," Doc assured him while dismounting. He beckoned Jesse. "Feed and water and, if you have time, a rubdown."

"Be right proud to tend such an elegant critter," grinned Jesse.

He led the bay to the barn. Accepting the Cobb's invitation to join them inside, Doc did so, mentally recoiling from the look of the kitchen, but encouraged by the aromas wafting from the stove at which Ma and her daughter now got to work. Because the other men were in shirtsleeves, he deemed it polite to follow their example; as well as hanging up his hat and duster, he removed his frockcoat. Slowly, laboriously, Dora Sue lowered herself to a chair. Cobb urged the guest be seated while Dora Sue sat gawking at the guest's multi-colored, silk-faced vest.

Cobb was all curiosity, What was Mr Beaumont's line of business?

"Professional gambler," Doc informed him. "We are also known as the sporting gentry."

"Oh, sure," nodded Cobb. "That'll be why you're headed for Sawyerville. I hear tell they got gamblin' houses there."

Doc consulted his watch and enquired, "May I hope to reach Sawyerville some time tonight?"

"On a fine horse like yours, I reckons you could," said Cobb. "'Fore sundown even."

"That would be most satisfactory," said Doc. Cobb was staring at his right hip. He rose, apologizing. "Your pardon, ladies, that I neglected to hang my sidearm before seating myself."

They stared at the weapon he hung by the door, an ebony-butted, nickel-plated Colt .45 housed in an ornately-tooled holster fixed to a well-stocked shellbelt. Jesse clumped in when his mother and sister were loading plates, paused to gape at the Colt and enthused, "By dawg, a gunfighter!"

"Mister Beaumont's a sportin' gent, boy," said Cobb. "That's a respectable profession and him and his kind got a right to protect 'emselves."

"For that purpose only, I travel armed," Doc assured everybody.

"Eatin' time," mumbled Ma Cobb.

"That purty horse, he's restin' easy in the corral now, mister," offered Jesse. "He was cool when I fed and watered him. You all right, Dora Sue, honey?"

"Aw, well," sighed Dora Sue. "You know."

During the meal, young Viola Cobb showed as much interest in Doc's fancy vest as did her sister-in-law. The cuisine was humdrum, but then the guest was hungry and willing to make do. For courtesy's sake, he kept his irritation well concealed. Lord, how he hated to compromise his high standards. These people, simpletons all of them, insular, reclusive, ignorant of the world beyond the few acres of dirt they tilled. How could anybody, no matter how humble their origins, be content to live this way?

Luncheon conversation was less than scintilating. Cobb bragged of his expectations of a good crop of corn; his beets and the other greens in the vegetable patch were coming along fine too. Doc congratulated him. Jesse asked if poker was a hard game to learn. Doc promptly advised him against taking lessons. Viola confided to him her big ambition. When she was old enough, *she'd* have a baby. Her brother reminded her she would have to get a husband first; that was how these things worked. Doc forced himself to play the gallant and remarked he was sure a young lady of Viola's quality was already aware of that fact.

The dessert, the inevitable apple pie, was to his taste. He complimented Ma on her cuisine and won blank stares. None of these peasants had heard the word 'cuisine' before, he realized.

"Fine apple pie," he translated.

"Ma's apple pie's as great as her coffee," Jesse assured him

That was a damn lie. Doc resisted the impulse to say it, and loudly, after his first sip of that muddy concoction. But he forced it down and was about to offer his host one of his Havana cigars when the totally unexpected happened. The Cobbs heard hoofbeats.

"Ain't that somethin'!" gasped the homesteader.

"More visitors — more company!" his son said in wonderment. "I'll be dawged! We *never* get company!" He rose eagerly. "Folks comin' and goin'!"

He hurried out to greet the riders, whose names were Mulhauser, Stack and Pacey. Cobb moved to a window. Viola and her mother hurried to the open doorway.

Jesse wasn't given time to voice a greeting. The three had reined up. As soon as he was in earshot, Mulhauser bluntly announced, "We're here for a saddle-critter."

"Mine's gettin' colicky I figure," growled Pacey.

"Pow'ful sorry, gents," frowned Jesse. "We ain't got no horses for sellin'."

Pacey and Stack traded mirthless grins. And now Doc, having heard those harsh voices, was suddenly wary. He rose, politely suggested Ma and daughter stay clear of the doorway, took down his gunbelt and strapped it on; they were bug-eyed when he thonged his holster down. He watched and listened.

Pacey and Stack were chuckling.

The elder man aimed a look at Jesse that chilled his blood and declared, "We ain't buyin' — we're takin'." Brusquely, he gestured to the corral. "That bay'll do. Bring him out."

"But — I couldn't do that," protested Jesse. "Us Cobbs don't even own him. He belongs to our visitor."

Doc chose this moment to show himself. Stepping out into the sunlight, he said calmly, "I'm the visitor." The three lost interest in Jesse, turning in their saddles to appraise him. "No horses for sale here, especially mine. Try taking any of them — that would be horse theft — as I'm sure you realize."

Three pairs of eyes sized him up. Mulhauser muttered something. The other two nudged their mounts closer to his and, for a few moments, there was a mumbled exchange inaudible to Doc, Jesse and the people inside the house. Then, shrugging, the strangers turned their horses as though to leave.

Pacey's move was fast. As he drew

and turned in his saddle, Doc whipped out his Colt and yelled to the frozen Jesse.

"Get down!"

Jesse threw himself flat as Pacey's gun boomed. Cursing in fluent French, lurching from the impact of the slug creasing his left side, Doc returned fire, heard Pacey's gasp of pain and saw a blur of blood in his upper right arm. Pacey didn't drop his weapon; he was jolted, but managed to stay mounted. Stack also had turned and Doc gave him no time to draw a bead. His Colt roared again and Stack was suddenly bareheaded, wailing in shock with his drilled hat spinning through the air.

Mulhauser snarled a command which was promptly obeyed. Doc sent another bullet after the three as they sank spur and took off at speed. He anticipated Cobb would have cut loose from the window with a shotgun, but decided this was too much to expect from these homesteaders; a lot of gaping, no action.

"You'll find a small black valise in my packroll," he growled at Jesse, now picking himself up — and still gawking. "Mister Cobb, the bathroom?"

"Well — uh — out back we got a . . . " began Cobb.

"Take me there," ordered Doc, holstering his pistol. "Boy, fetch that valise!"

Cobb emerged and led him around back. There were two out-houses, one a privy, the other the family's only ablution facility. While he stripped to the waist, Cobb pumped water into a clean — Doc hoped — dish. His son arrived with Doc's black bag, still in a dazed condition, mumbling.

"By dawg, you're plenty slick with that six-shooter, Mister Beaumont."

"Not fast enough this time!" fumed Doc. "Drat the scum. One of them grazed me."

He stayed on his feet, immersed a clean handkerchief in the bowl and swabbed and inspected his wound. Not too deep, a shallow crease, and not bleeding now. He took his bag from Jesse, opened it and delved for a bottle of antiseptic, a small pot of balm and the wherewithal for fashioning and taping a dressing.

Father and son followed his deft movements in mute fascination. Not until Doc was redonning his upper garments did Jesse regain the power of speech.

"You ain't a gamblin' man! You're a real doc!"

"That is my secret and I'll thank you to keep it," Doc said sternly.

"I don't savvy why you lied to us," frowned Cobb.

"I do not lie, sir!" snapped Doc. "I prefer poker to the practice of medicine. I never mention all my qualifications. That is *not* lying. I am merely protecting my right to privacy."

"Maybe that makes some kinda sense," Cobb conceded. "Come to think of it, I once knew a blacksmith used to preach at Sunday church meetin's."

"Life's sure gettin' lively round here, Pa," remarked Jesse. "Many a month since anybody happened by and, in one hour, we get company for lunch and three horse thieves and a shootin' fight. Hot damn!"

"I'm leaving now," Doc informed them. "After which I've no doubt you'll resume your bucolic existence in perfect tranquility."

They were moving into the rear yard, passing the vegetable plot, when a shriek blasted their ears.

"Hey, that's Dora Sue a'hollerin'!" cried Jesse.

"All that shootin' — too much excitement for her," opined his father.

Doc groaned inwardly. This was too much. A warlike return of the horse thieves, another shoot-out with them, would be infinitely preferable to what he feared was about to happen, not to mention easier on his nerves.

"Her time's come!" yelled Jesse, bee-lining for the house.

Of all the duties of a physician, the

one Doc most resented was childbirth. Expectant mothers and fathers were low on his list of favourite people; he hated the hassle of it all, the jumping nerves of next of kin invariably getting under his feet, the general air of suspense, the fussing and fretting. Indeed, his antipathy for maternity cases had been a major motive for his abandoning medicine. He had never established a practice, never hung out a shingle, and never would.

He was about to detour toward the corral and barn when he remembered his hat and coat, also his duster, were in the kitchen. And, besides, Cobb was grasping his arm.

"You can't leave now!" protested the homesteader.

"Watch my dust," growled Doc.

"But you're a doc and she's gonna birth," argued Cobb. "Ma never midwifed another woman before, only critters. Viola dunno nothin', me and my boy neither." He followed Doc into the kitchen. "Take too long to fetch a doc from Sawyerville. You gotta tend her. It's — it's your Christian duty."

"Am I to be spared nothing?" groaned Doc.

Viola came scuttling through a side doorway.

"We put her to bed!" she breathlessly announced. "She's squawkin' terrible and — and I gotta boil up some water!"

"And *you* gotta . . . " began Cobb.

"Great balls of fire!" raged Doc.

"Thisaway," urged Cobb.

Dora Sue would play her role for all it was worth. This was at once obvious to Doc when he entered the untidy bedroom. Hands clasped to swollen belly, she rocked back and forth on the bed and wailed in anguish, while her mother-in-law stood wringing her hands and her distraught husband tried to soothe her by grasping her shoulders probably hard enough to inflict severe bruising, it seemed to Doc.

"Silence!" he ordered. "Mrs Cobb, you may remain — provided you do not impede my examination. You . . . !" He pointed to the sweating father-to-be. "Out! Go chop firewood!"

"We got plenty firewood," said Cobb.

"Chop more!" Doc snarled at Jesse. "Take an axe, find timber — a mile from here would be fine — and don't return until you're sent for."

Intimidated, Jesse, his father and sister left him to it. He moved to the bed, set his bag down and growled at Dora Sue to lie still.

"You're a — regular doctor — Jesse said," frowned Ma.

"I am, madam," he nodded. "But, right now I wish I were a stagecoach driver. I have to make an examination. Can you take her hand and persuade her to *cease that infernal din*?" As he began, he asked, "Has she come her full term?"

"Done what?" blinked Ma.

He rephrased the question through clenched teeth.

"Is this her ninth month?"

"Oh, well and truly," Ma assured him. "She's ready."

"She may believe so," he retorted. "Whether or not the *babe's* ready to arrive is the important factor."

All he could ascertain from his examination was that Dora Sue Cobb was certainly in labor, and this was no indication of the time element. He fervently hoped it would be a short labor.

Ma applied cold compresses and murmured encouragingly. Exasperated, Doc retreated to the kitchen for a much-needed smoke. Cobb demanded, as he lit his cigar, "What's happenin'?"

Doc answered his question with a question.

"Have you ever heard of false labor?"

"Sure I have," bragged Cobb. "I ain't all that iggerant."

"Then you'll be aware your daughter-in-law is experiencing what could be called a rehearsal for the main event," said Doc.

"But it could start again any time,"

insisted Cobb. "Any time from now on."

"That is invariably the case," Doc dryly assured him.

"So you gotta stay," declared Cobb.

"You've forgotten I have business in Sawyerville," chided Doc.

"Sure you got business elsewhere," nodded Cobb. "But what in tarnation could any of us do when she starts calvin'? Hell Doc, she could up and die on us, her and the baby too. You can't just ride out of here now. You gotta *wait*."

Doc thought about three high rollers, chickens for the plucking in Sawyerville, and cursed his luck. On the one hand, he prided himself on his utter indifference to lesser mortals encountered during his troubles. On the other had, that damn-blasted Hippocratic oath haunted him like the ghost of an ancestor he'd as soon forget, but couldn't. This was a textbook maternity case, but had any Cobb read the textbook — always assuming they *could* read? Without a qualified medical practitioner on hand, this birth could be a king-sized shambles.

It was one of those times. He was stuck. He couldn't ride away from this.

"If you know any prayers . . . " he sighed.

"Why wouldn't we?" challenged Cobb. "This here's a Christian family. We should pray for Dora Sue you mean?"

"For me," corrected Doc. "Pray she'll come into labor again within the hour and that, this time, we'll achieve the routine result. Then I may be fortunate enough to see Sawyerville *some* time tonight."

Toward sundown, while the gambling medico from New Orleans was still waiting it out, the Texans and Slow Wolf entered Sawyerville from the south. As seen through their optimistic eyes, this cattle town looked good for an overnight stay, a big place, but orderly.

The stablehand at Sutton's Livery was part-Indian and offered no objection to

Slow Wolf's bunking in the hayloft. Out of earshot of this obliging character, the pudgy redman assured his tall friends, "My needs are simple. I'll be comfortable enough here. May I suggest, if you have sufficient funds, you avail yourself of the facilities of a hotel."

No problem. At games of chance, Lady Luck smiled on the trouble-shooters more often than not; their joint bankroll tallied to some $500 at this time.

From Sutton's Livery to the Duffield Hotel they toted their gear. The desk clerk checked them into a second-floor double and, after stashing packrolls, saddlebags and sheathed Winchesters, they descended to the dining-room for supper.

Now they were in Colorado, but still some distance from the Rockies and the hunting and fishing they craved. Again, no problem. Time was what they had plenty of, as Stretch reminded his partner.

They scorned Sawyerville's houses of entertainment in favor of an early night and, by 9.30, were in their room again, flipping a dime to decide on their choice of beds. Larry won the bed closest the window and, within the half-hour, both drifters were deep in slumber.

Not till dawn of the next day, coincidentally about the same time Doc Beaumont was ushering a new Cobb into this world, were Sawyerville County's lawmen stirred to action.

It began when Janet Jupp, wife of local storekeeper, awoke to discover her husband's side of the bed had not been slept in; his pillow showed no impression. At first, as she rose to don bathrobe and slippers, she was merely curious. But, when she descended from their living quarters into the store . . .

4

The Sawyerville Scene

BECAUSE the front window shades were drawn, Janet Jupp did not immediately sight her hapless spouse. She moved to the windows, raised the shades, then checked the street door. Unlocked. That was unusual and certainly careless of David. He always locked up before retiring. But then he hadn't actually retired, had he?

She turned, and now her husband was clearly visible, roped to a chair, gagged and with a livid bruise on his brow. His eyes were open, his expression eloquent; but for his gag, he'd have been urging her to free him of his bonds.

She intended doing so, naturally, but first opened the street door and loosed a scream, figuring this was how a lady should react in such circumstances. The scream was heard by Deputy Sheriff Slim Moore on his way home from having worked the midnight to sun-up patrol. Moore was weary, but changed direction and bee-lined for Jupp's General Mercantile.

When he hustled in, Janet had rid her husband of the gag and was untying him — and he was in good voice.

"Thieving sons of bitches!" he raged. "Three of 'em, Slim. I let 'em in after I closed up. Well, an extra sale I thought, you know?"

"You let 'em in, then what?" demanded Moore.

"Then it was too late," complained Dave Jupp. "They were masked. Bandannas. And pointing guns at me. The wild-eyed one vowed he'd blow my head off if I raised a rumpus. The bareheaded one helped himself to a pearl-grey Stetson and they started filling a sack with — all kinds of supplies — and then one of 'em found the cashbox. That's when I got mad. I'd have hollered, but I got clobbered by a gun. When I woke up, I was trussed to the chair and — I couldn't make anybody hear!"

Janet held up the empty cashbox, its lid prised from its hinges.

"Five days' of trading — all gone," she told the deputy. "Dave would've banked it today."

"This happened . . . ?" prodded Moore.

"About eight-thirty last night," Jupp recalled. "Damn it, Slim. Five days' take. You got to do something!"

"Do the best we can, Dave, but you have to face up to it," said Moore. "They've had time on their side, more than time enough to get far clear of the county line." As he turned to leave, he thought to ask, "You need a doctor?"

"Hell, no, my brains aren't scrambled," mumbled Jupp. "I calculate I came to my senses about ten minutes after I was clobbered." After the deputy left, he shrugged helplessly and hooked an arm about his wife's waist. "You're a great wife — haven't I always said it? But how I wish you were a light sleeper."

Moore trudged in again, knuckling at his eyes.

"So blame weary — I'm getting forgetful," he grouched. "Didn't get a description."

"The skunk that stole the pearl-grey hat was fair-haired," offered Jupp. "He stood about so high." He raised a hand. "There was a heavyset feller and the older one . . . " Grimacing nervously, he worked on his memory again. "He was about six foot tall, a scarecrow with — uh — with crazy eyes."

"Crazy eyes?" frowned Moore.

"Like he hates every mother's son in the whole damn world," declared Jupp. "And they were the shabbiest bunch I've seen in a long time — real bad bastards. Sorry, Jan honey, but . . . "

"Five days' take," she complained. "Cuss 'em all you want."

No sooner had Moore quit the

emporium than he was confronted by the indignant Lee Walter, proprietor of Walter's Square Deal Livery Stable, who furiously announced, "I've been robbed!"

"It's starting to sound like it was a busy night for robbers," winced Moore. "All right, Lee, I'm listening."

"*My* horse they stole!" raged Walter. "My strawberry roan, my own personal saddle-animal! He's gone from his stall, my stablehand's head's all busted — I already sent my wife to fetch Doc Whitehead — and what do you suppose they left in Big Red's stall? A horse with colic!"

"That's adding insult to injury," Moore sympathized. He darted a glance uptown and saw his boss and the other deputy entering an early opening diner. "All right, Mister Walter, I'll report to Sheriff Ilford rightaway. We'll take prompt action, but I can't make any promises."

At least he could down a cup of black coffee at Stanley's Diner, he was thinking as he headed in that direction. Wasn't this a pain in the ass? Two robberies reported to him within minutes of his finishing the graveyard shift. He craved sleep, but business was business, especially the law enforcement business.

Thanks to the color of his thick thatch, any local or transient of average intelligence could guess why Sheriff Augustus Ilford was nicknamed Rusty Gus. He was bulky and aging, a durable lawman, conscientious, but of placid disposition. His breakfast companion was his other deputy, Curly Fuller. Fuller had worked the sundown to midnight patrol and was looking so clear-eyed, so alert at this moment that Moore could cheerfully have strangled him.

Joining his fellow star-toters, he sagged into a chair, begged the waitress to fetch him a whole pot of black coffee and reported both robberies adding the storekeeper's description of his assailants and the color of Walter's missing horse, which Ilford and Fuller knew anyway.

"Chances are they stole the strawberry roan before they hit the Jupp store," was the sheriff's comment.

"During your shift," Moore told Fuller.

"Right, yes, no question about that," Fuller said briskly. "So they worked quietly and patiently, must have. When I'm on patrol duty — you know this, Gus — I stay sharp and keep my eyes peeled, but what we got here is a big town. I can't be . . . "

"In a dozen different places at the same time," nodded Ilford. "To me, you sometimes seem to be, but that's because you're so fast on your feet."

Moore's coffee arrived. He gulped at it desperately.

"Not much chance they're still here, Gus," he muttered. "And I know what you're gonna say."

"And you know it's true," said Ilford. "Comes to scouting for tracks and miscreants, you're better at it than

Curly. Comes to checking hotels and doss-houses — in case they *are* still here — Curly's better at that than you."

"Fast on my feet," bragged Fuller.

"A bellyful of that coffee'll keep you going, Slim," said Ilford. "You can stay awake long enough to scout the area beyond town. You know what to look for, track of three riders headed for any of the county borders."

After his third refill of coffee, Moore grudgingly heaved himself upright.

He complained, as he turned to leave, "Sometimes I wish I'd gotten into some other business, a bookstore'd suit me fine."

When his senior deputy had left, Ilford urged his junior deputy, "Eat fast, then hustle around town and ask questions. Any strangers you hear of, check 'em."

"Right, I'll do that," Fuller assured him. "Just leave it with me, Gus."

A short time later, he was bustling into the Jupp store to express his regrets that Jupp's head still ached and to ask if he could add any details to his description of the robbers.

"Any little thing you can remember, Dave. Mole on a feller's nose, crooked teeth, scar on his chin anything like that."

"They had bandannas pulled right up to their eyes," Jupp reminded him.

"Right, yes, I understand," nodded Fuller. "So other details? How about the way they talked?"

"Rough," said Jupp.

"Rough," Fuller thoughtfully repeated. "How about accents? Could any of 'em be Mexican, for instance?"

"They were three white men, three thieving skunks, and that's all I can tell you," said Jupp.

"Tall?" prodded Fuller.

"The tallest was a six-footer," recalled Jupp. "He's the one with the crazy eyes. Scared hell out of me."

"He couldn't've been a little less than six feet, or a little more?" asked Fuller. "I need a clear picture."

"He didn't give me time to measure

him, but I'm saying six feet exactly and now my head's aching worse than when you came in," groaned Jupp.

"Sorry about that, Dave," said Fuller, retreating to the doorway. "I'll get into this rightaway."

Having decided to canvass livery stables before checking hotels, Fuller hurried into Sutton's Livery soon afterward to find two half-breeds sharing a cornmeal breakfast. He nodded to the stablehand and addressed Slow Wolf.

"Savvy English?" he demanded.

"Some," said Slow Wolf.

"You're a stranger, but that's okay because you aren't a paleface," decided Fuller.

"You heap smart lawman," the stablehand remarked poker-faced. "Don't miss much."

"Name?" asked Fuller.

"Elmer Red Sky," said the stablehand.

"Not you, Elmer," said Fuller, "Him."

"Me Slow Wolf."

"Right, fine, I got that. Now, Slow

Wolf, when you come to Sawyerville?"

"Sundown."

"Yesterday, huh? Good. You happen to see three palefaces?"

The stablehand, Elmer Red Sky, felt he should remind the deputy, "What else he see but whites? Me only redman in town."

"You got a point, Elmer," Fuller was quick to agree. "But three palefaces together, Slow Wolf, one of 'em with crazy eyes?" Slow Wolf shook his head. "Fine. You honest Injun?"

"Speak straight," Slow Wolf gravely assured him.

Satisfied, the agile Deputy Fuller resumed his runaround, which eventually brought him to the Duffield Hotel. Questioned as to new arrivals, the desk clerk informed him two strangers had checked in early yesterday evening. As they had not yet come down for breakfast, he would find them in Room 15 upstairs.

Fuller climbed the stairs three at a time, proceeded to the door numbered 15, knocked and entered and appraised Messrs Valentine and Emerson, barefoot and naked but for the towels wrapped about their midsections. They were shaving.

"You're in the clear," he decided. "Too tall, even barefoot."

With that, he pulled a fast disappearing trick. The Texans frowned at the closed door, still plying their razors.

"Quick visit," Stretch remarked.

"Fast on his feet," said Larry. "I scarce had time to notice he's a badge-toter."

"Well, we're in the clear he said," drawled Stretch. "Ain't that a comfort?"

"Uh huh," grunted Larry. "We're too tall."

"Even barefoot," nodded Stretch.

They finished shaving, dressed and descended to the Duffield's dining-room for breakfast while Deputy Fuller pursued his enquires, darting in and out of every hotel in town, questioning passers-by. A very busy deputy was Curly Fuller, as was the other deputy, the yawning Moore, now scouting the terrain east of the county seat.

Having delivered Dora Sue Cobb of an eight and a half pounds son and partaken of an indifferent breakfast, Doc Beaumont was ready to take his leave of the homesteaders. He was in need of sleep, but willing to ride weary rather than spend five more minutes with the Cobbs.

They thanked him profusely after he strapped on his Colt and donned frockcoat and duster. Jesse reported he had saddled the bay and secured his gear.

"We'll never forget you," Cobb warmly declared.

"Please do," retorted Doc. "I hate to be remembered."

"It was a decent Christian thing you did for our Dora Sue," said Ma.

"You were so clever," Viola said admiringly. "I dunno how you did it."

"It is not exactly a new and exciting medical procedure," scowled

Doc. "Goes back to the beginning of time in fact."

"Dora Sue's feelin' right fine now, little Jesse too," grinned the proud father. "And, the way it turned out, I didn't need to go chop all that wood."

"Yes, you did," said Doc.

He moved out to his waiting horse with Jesse tagging him, still irritating him with his bragging. Fatherhood was the greatest thing that had ever happened to him, he kept repeating. As far as Doc was concerned, he was welcome.

About to raise boot to stirrup, he paused to stare. Nobody had thought to remove an item left over from his brief exchange of shots with three heavily armed scavengers.

Jesse followed his glance.

"That's the hat," he said somewhat unnecessarily. "The hat you shot right off of that jasper's head."

"Bring it to me," ordered Doc.

Jesse obeyed. Then, watching the

New Orleans dandy secure it to his gear, he waxed inquisitive.

"What you gonna do with it?"

"Return it to its owner eventually — I sincerely hope," Doc said grimly.

He nudged the bay to movement and started for the east trail without a backward glance, though the Cobbs were still wishing him well — at the top of their voices.

Mid-morning in Sawyerville, Deputy Moore returned to report to his chief. A southbound stage was departing just as he looped his rein to the law office hitch rail. Ilford was seated at his desk, about to open official correspondence just delivered. He motioned his senior deputy to a chair, but the office couch was Moore's immediate destination. He sagged onto it and the sheriff urged him, "Just perch, Slim. Don't lie down. I'd as soon you talk before you pass out."

"Cut their sign," yawned Moore.

"Three riders?" prodded Ilford.

"Three," said Moore. "Tagged 'em

to our east border."

"They'll be the three who visited the Square Deal livery and the Jupp store," Ilford opined. "Gone from my jurisdiction now, well-provisioned, one of 'em wearing a new hat, one of 'em riding Lee Walter's strawberry roan." He swore swiftly. "They got away with more than robbery."

"Uh . . . ?" Moore was yawning again.

"Murder," scowled Ilford. "I got word a little while ago. Walter's stablehand didn't make it, died of his head-wound."

"Hell," breathed Moore.

"I'll wire the descriptions — such as they are — to the nearest law authorities east, north and south," said Ilford. "Nothing else I can do about those marauders. And no use blaming Curly. It's a big town. He'd have been three or four blocks away when they did their dirty work. Maybe this'll stir the mayor and his council pals to action. For a year or more, I've been warning them I need at least one extra deputy, also a jailer. There's just too much of Sawyerville to be patrolled by one deputy after dark. Slim, are you listening?" Moore's head was lolling. He raised his voice before his senior deputy could begin snoring. "On your feet, Slim!"

"I'm trying — I'm trying . . . " mumbled Moore.

He made it upright after some effort.

"Now go home and sleep," urged Ilford.

Moore needed no second bidding.

Over breakfast, the Texans learned the reason for an agile deputy's in-again-out-again visit to their room just by eavesdropping on the conversation of other guests. There had been more than a little excitement in town pre-midnight, the theft of a horse from a livery stable, fortunately not the Sutton establishment, the slaying of a stablehand, the gunwhipping and robbing of a storekeeper.

"And it seemed like a good peaceable

town when we rode in," muttered Stretch.

"Look, that couldn've been the most trouble they've had here in a year or more," reasoned Larry. "Now it's over and we're sorry about the dead stablehand, but we'll let the local law fret about it. That's what they're paid for."

"Ain't that the truth," Stretch agreed. "We ain't here to poke our snoots into law business."

"We'll just rest a while, pick up a few supplies and then, say mid-afternoon, us and the Chief'll head for the high country," said Larry. "We've had our bellyful of huntin' bandidos. I'm in a mood for huntin' what's good to eat; deer, quail, whatever we can shoot in the mountains."

"I'm with you," Stretch assured him. "But, while we're here, we might's well look the town over, huh? Kind of stretch our legs?"

Early afternoon of this day, if any locals thought them an odd trio, two tough-looking hombres in range clothes and a flabby redman in buckskin sharing a sidewalk bench, they kept their curiosity to themselves. One of the strangers, though, a lazy-looking character, packed twice as much Colt as his partner. People sensed Stretch's second .45 was no showpiece, and they were right; with handguns he was ambidextrous.

Slow Wolf and his friends were just taking it easy until they sighted the lone rider making a slow approach from the north, just now entering Main Street.

"Well," grinned Stretch. "Will you look who's here."

"Ah, the refined and brilliant Doctor Vincent Beaumont," observed Slow Wolf. "Physician, poker addict and surgeon extraordinaire."

He and Stretch were puzzled when Larry said abruptly, "I don't want him to sight us. C'mon, let's move."

When he quit the bench and sidled eight feet to his right into an alley-mouth, they followed, still confused.

Joining him there, they gave vent to their curiosity.

"Hey, runt, he always gets mad at us when we run into him, no argument about that . . . " began Stretch.

"What an irony that is," mused Slow Wolf. "You admire him so much, he claims to despise you. Yet, in so many perilous situations, you have fought side by side."

"This time we're gonna give him a break and stay clear of him," declared Larry. "It's what he always wants anyway."

"You gettin' soft?" challenged Stretch. "Every other time, it's a big laugh for us, him cussin' us, you and me joshin' him."

"Poke your head out — do it careful so he won't see you," instructed Larry. "Take a good look at him."

The bay was toting Doc along Main — slowly. Stretch watched him pass, watched him move on toward Sawyerville's biggest gambling house, Butler's Palace, then withdrew his head and frowned at his partner.

"Doc don't look so good, looks plumb toilworn," he said.

"I noticed," nodded Larry.

"You are keen-sighted, friend Lawrence," remarked Slow Wolf.

"Minute I recognized him, I guessed things ain't right for him," said Larry. To Stretch, he opined, "This mightn't be a good time for us to fool with him. We oughtn't forget we owe him."

"We've saved his hide many a time," argued Stretch.

"Sure," shrugged Larry. "But remember Delarno way up in Oregon? We were shot up bad, could've died in that town. And Doc just happened to be there. It was him tended our wounds."

"Ain't about to forget that," frowned Stretch. "We were just about done for that time."

"Now and then, I get a twinge in some parts of my carcass, just to remind me," said Larry.

"You and me both," nodded Stretch.

"So we ain't gonna faze him? Well, that's fair, I guess. We've always riled Doc, but we've never treated him cruel." He winced as he asked, "You afeared he's hurtin'? Sick maybe?"

"I'd like to know for sure," said Larry.

Slow Wolf modestly reminded him, "I have the advantage of being somewhat nondescript, also discreet. If you wish . . ."

"Yeah, you're good at that," recalled Larry.

"Snoopin' and spyin'," said Stretch.

"I prefer the word surveillance," protested Slow Wolf. "You, my good friends, express concern for another good friend. I will, if you so desire, keep him under observation in my own unobtrusive way."

"Muchas gracias, Chief, you do that," begged Larry. "Anything you find out, come tell us. We're in Room fifteen at the Duffield Hotel."

"Goin' back there now, are we?" asked Stretch.

"Might's well rest our bones till Slow Wolf's got somethin' to tell us," decided Larry.

Doc was clinging to his hopes, which were soon to be dashed, when he entered the luxuriously appointed barroom of Butler's Palace. Only the blackjack and faro tables were drawing trade from optimists in the sector to his left reserved for games of chance. No poker tables were in use at this time. Fearing the worst, he moved to the blue-gowned woman on duty at the roulette layout. She had no clients.

He greeted her in his courtly manner. She identified herself only by her first name, Eve.

"You can perhaps advise me as to whether three sporting gentlemen, Merrill Peters and his friends, are still in town," he suggested.

"Stayed a couple of weeks, a lot of high stake poker parties while they were here," she informed him. "Gone now. Left on the southbound stage just this morning."

Doc thanked her for this information while secretly cursing the gunmen responsible for his prolonged stay at the Cobb homestead, as well as the smarting of his wound. To pursue the stage was out of the question. His horse wasn't weary, but *he* certainly was. At the moment, he was thinking as a doctor, not a gambler, admitting to himself that, though his wound had not bled profusely, there had been some loss of blood. That and lack of sleep at the homestead had left him near exhausted.

"Another question, if you'd be so kind," he said.

"Ask me anything," invited the lady known as Eve.

"Best hotel in town?" he enquired.

"Miller's Alhambra," was her prompt recommendation. "Big and easy to find, three-storey place corner of Main and Dalton."

He doffed his hat to her and was on his way out when a dapper local, obviously another professional gambler, fell in beside him.

"Couldn't help overhearing, friend," he said "Hawke's the name, Pawley Hawke. Big disappointment, the departure of Peters and those other high rollers, Mister . . . ?"

"Beaumont," Doc offered as they made their exit. He stood by the hitch rail, making no secret of his chagrin. "It was my earnest hope to join them here. An all-night game would have been enjoyable, profitable too."

"You don't have to feel so disappointed," said Hawke, grinning encouragingly. "Still plenty action to be had in Sawyerville, mostly at Herb Conklin's place." He gestured southward. "Last place downtown. The Even Break it's called, and I personally recommend it. Always a high-stake game to be had there."

"Sounds promising," Doc commented. "I may look in this evening."

"Just one thing," cautioned Hawke. "Don't be put off by the look of the Even Break. Conklin doesn't favor fancy appointments and expensive furnishing like you saw in here. He caters to gentlemen gamblers who appreciate good liquor and a square game. The Even Break has really earned its name, so who cares if it looks a mite rundown?"

"Appearances aren't that important," agreed Doc. "Well, thank you, Hawke. I'll be there tonight."

"Fine," nodded Hawke. "I wouldn't take my business anywhere else, so we'll probably find ourselves at the same table."

The New Orleans man stabled his mount at the Walter barn and toted his gear to Sawyerville's best hotel, where the desk clerk had him sign the register and checked him into an upstairs suite. Only the best for Doc Beaumont. A mere bedroom with a wash basin? Totally inadequate. He requested and was assigned a suite comprising bedroom, parlor and private bathroom.

When he descended after unpacking,

he had discarded his duster. The clerk listened to his question and directed him to Maurice Harvey's establishment.

"A block uptown on the east side of Main, Mister Beaumont. Finest gents' clothing store in Sawyerville, nothing but high-quality stock and patronized only by better class citizens."

Some short time later, the desk clerk of another hotel, the Duffield, knocked on the door of Room 15 and, when Larry opened it, eyed him uncertainly.

"Excuse me," he said. "Do you have a friend — who's an *Indian*?"

Stretch joined his partner in the doorway. The clerk still wore his bemused expression; their faces were inscrutable.

"Depends," said Larry. "This Injun got a name?"

"Called himself Slow Wolf and asked for you," frowned the clerk.

"Oh, him?" shrugged Stretch. "He's my grandfather."

The clerk sighed heavily and complained, "One of my legs is suddenly aching. I think it's being pulled."

"You don't need to be leery of our Injun buddy," Larry assured him. "He's plumb harmless."

"What day is this?" asked Stretch.

"Tuesday," said the clerk.

"You got nothin' to worry about," soothed Stretch. "Slow Wolf's kind of set in his ways, never scalps nobody on Tuesdays."

"Now you know why I avoid getting into fights," the clerk said as they accompanied him downstairs. "I always lead with my chin." When they reached the lobby, he gestured to the entrance. "He's out there on the porch."

The drifters joined Slow Wolf by the porch rail. No stone-faced redman was he. His eyes were doleful right now.

"Our friend, the good doctor, is staying at what must be the finest hotel in this town, the Alhambra," he muttered. "At least I presume so, for I followed him from there to a store."

"Real fancy gents' store I bet," drawled Stretch. "Doc always did favor high-class duds."

"Just such a store, yes," nodded Slow Wolf. "I watched — discreetly of course — from a side window. He replaced three garments, his undershirt, his shirt and his vest. And donned his purchases there in the store. Very smart, the vest. Of checked pattern and colorful, but in good taste."

"Redman speaks with ramblin' tongue," complained Larry. "C'mon, Chief, make your point."

"The items he discarded were blood-stained," said Slow Wolf.

"Damn!" breathed Stretch. "Seems your hunch was right, runt."

"I don't believe his wound is critical — he moves easily, albeit slowly," frowned Slow Wolf. "But wounded he undoubtedly is. I glimpsed a dressing. Left side."

"All right," said Larry. "I call that a good enough reason for us to stay out of his way."

"Wouldn't be kindly of us," agreed Stretch. "Joshin' Doc while he's hurtin'."

Joseph Whitehead, M.D., eldest of Sawyer County's resident physicians, had no patients at this time, just a visitor. He and Sheriff Ilford were of similar age. They were sharing a seat on the front porch of the medic's home, discussing the wanton slaying of Lon Finley, the stablehand who had fallen victim to the horse thieves.

"I kept the telegrapher busy, Joe," Ilford said, while his friend filled and lit a bent-stemmed brier. "Wired the U.S. Marshal's office at Denver even, as well as the sheriffs of areas east of here, Sillsburg, Ashcroft, Perdido."

"You optimistic?" asked Whitehead.

"Not one little bit," grouched Ilford. "Country's too big, Joe. Think of all the hideaway holes in the high country. I get angry just thinking of it, the idea they'll stay free after what they did to Lonny, Dave Jupp, the horse stealing, the looting. But that's how it'll be. They'll get away with it."

"You aren't your usual calm self today," observed Whitehead. "Well, who could blame you?"

"Jupp's the lucky one," reflected Ilford. "He lost cash and stock, but that bump on his head . . . "

"Hard blow, enough to render him unconscious, but not for long," said Whitehead. "Finley's the big loser. A savage beating he took. In a way, it's a mercy he didn't survive. There'd have been brain damage, Gus. He'd have been — just an automaton." He puffed on his pipe a while. "I take it Jupp's description of the guilty parties was of little help?"

"There's one possibility," confided Ilford. He was thinking of the correspondence he had checked through before visiting the medico. "I've had word of the release of a long-termer from the Daggart Penitentiary."

"Long way from here," frowned Whitehead. "Up by the Nevada-Oregan border, isn't it?"

"Even so," said Ilford. "After so long inside, what does the released man need? Cash, provisions, transportation.

And this particular feller was no model prisoner, a real wild one, maybe . . . " He raised a finger to his temple, "more than a mite touched."

"All the way from North Nevada?" challenged Whitehead.

"It might not be such a far-fetched notion," said Ilford. "One detail Jupp recalls about the robbers, the eyes of the tallest of his attackers. Wild, he says. Crazy eyes."

"Interesting," mused Whitehead.

"Why couldn't friends've been waiting for him when he was turned loose?" suggested Ilford. "Let's say two friends?"

"It's a theory," said Whitehead. "But of no use to you, since Deputy Moore reported they're long gone from Sawyer County."

"I know it won't be me nails the wild-eyed one," sighed Ilford. "Maybe Mulhauser will never be nailed. That's his name, Carl Mulhauser. But, if he's the one stove Finley's head in, I wish it could happen. I liked Lon Finley."

"Yes," said Whitehead. "Harmless

he was, no trouble to anybody, just a plodder. And the plodders are so often the victims, aren't they? It's a cruel life for some, Gus."

Ilford got to his feet.

"Best be getting back to my office," he decided. "See you around, Joe."

"Back to business for me too," Whitehead said as he knocked dottle from his pipe. The hinges of his front gate squeaked; a patient arriving. "Here comes Brice McColley. That dyspeptic condition of his just won't quit."

While Ilford was crossing Main to return to his office, two more strangers were arriving, moving in from the north, a big man on a handsome black accompanied by a disreputable-looking, pint-sized Mexican.

5

Some Men You Don't Forget

FROM the outskirts, Jim Gage surveyed several blocks of Sawyerville's main street. In the 4 p.m. sunlight, the county seat appeared impressive.

"They will not be here, those hombres malo," mumbled Benito. "You know they came this way, but they are far ahead of you, amigo. Much distance is between you and them."

"I'm overnighting here," said Jim. "And I'll be talking to people. Somebody must've noticed 'em. Some men you don't forget." He was on the lookout for a a livery stable. "First we bed our horses. After that, I have to hope the lawmen of Sawyerville are as observant as they ought to be. I'll be paying a call on the sheriff."

"Gringo rurales," winced Benito.

"You're leery of the law — as you should be," chided Jim. "I guess you never heard the word kleptomaniac."

"Que?" blinked Benito.

"It's what you are," growled Jim. "If you're ever cured of your itchy-fingered condition, cucaracha, you'll be better company."

With his runt shadow tagging, he turned Junior toward the Sutton stable. They dismounted out front, led their mounts in and were greeted by the stablehand.

"How long, mister?" he asked.

"Just for tonight," Jim told him. "Fresh straw, feed, water and rubdown. And don't let anybody try to mount the black."

"*I* sure won't," frowned the stablehand. "Hey, isn't he broke?"

"Well and truly," nodded Jim. "You'll find him easy to handle. It's just he won't take any rider. Just me. Back later for our gear, okay?"

"Take your time," shrugged the stablehand.

Casually at first, Jim glanced at filled stalls. Then Benito noted his sudden interest, the way he moved to two stalls to study the occupants, a sorrel and pinto.

"You are curious again," he frowned.

Horses were the big man's business and, after his family, a constant preoccupation. With his eyes fixed on those two animals, he remarked, "It's been quite a time, but I could swear I've seen 'em before. How come they seem familiar? Well, it'll come to me." He turned away, enquiring of the stablehand, "Which way to the sheriff's office?"

The stablehand offered directions. Jim moved out with Benito, crossed the street and walked south. When they reached Sawyerville's headquarters of law and order, the little Mex sidled into the alley beside it, a move that caused Jim no surprise.

He entered to find the sheriff at his

desk and Slim Moore lounging in the open cellblock doorway. Ilford looked up and nodded affably.

"'Afternoon. Help you?"

"You might be able to," said Jim, offering his hand. "J. C. Gage from Nevada."

"Gus Ilford, county sheriff," nodded Ilford. "Deputy Sheriff Moore."

As they shook, Jim traded nods with the deputy. He took the chair indicated by the sheriff and came straight to the point.

"I've been trailing three men who must've passed through your town. One of 'em I can name. Mulhauser. And I can show you his picture."

The lawmen swapped quick glances. Moore asked, "Trailed 'em from where?"

"Cornerstone, my hometown up by the Humboldt River country," Jim told them. "I run a horse ranch in that territory."

"Calculating it roughly, you've followed Mulhauser and his companeros something like five hundred and fifty miles," frowned Ilford.

"A storm slowed me down, blew out all tracks," said Jim. "When I cut their sign again, I was led to a homestead north-west of here, family name of Cobb. They'd been there, tried to steal a horse. There was some shooting, because the Cobbs had a lunch guest and the thieves had their eyes on his mount, a bay."

"Owner of the bay fazed 'em off — all three of 'em?" challenged Moore.

"The Cobbs told me his name," said Jim. "He's a man I know and, yes, he could do that, send three hard cases running. Mostly he gambles, but he's quite a pistolero. The thing is, when they fled from the homestead, they crossed the border and came this way." He produced his wallet and a proffered the report he had torn from the Whitton Forks paper. "That's Mulhauser, and could that face be forgotten by any Sawyerville folk who sighted it?"

"Crazy eyes, Jupp said," Ilford

reminded the deputy.

"Jupp wasn't fooling," muttered Moore.

"So he was seen here?" prodded Jim.

"Unfortunately, not by either of my deputies, only by a storekeeper and a stablehand," scowled Ilford. "The storekeeper, Dave Jupp, is soreheaded and will clinch the identification I'm sure. We'd learn nothing from the stablehand. He was struck harder, a savage head blow — probably with a pistol barrel. He'll be buried tomorrow."

"They're long gone, Gage," said Moore. "I tagged tracks of three riders to the east county line."

"All right," said Jim. "I didn't expect they'd hang around anyway. I'll overnight here and head after 'em tomorrow morning."

"And your reason for hunting 'em?" demanded Ilford. "You carry no badge. You're a horse rancher — so it's personal?"

Jim told them how personal, recounting

his run-in with the three rogues and bluntly declaring he was in no doubt as to who had slain Hank. Ilford grimaced in disgust.

"Mean minds — real mean," commented Moore. "An ex-convict and his cronies take a licking from a man, and butchering his favorite horse is their idea of paying him off. Hell, Gus . . . "

"Uh huh," grunted Ilford. "They don't come any lower." He had not returned the strip of newspaper showing Mulhauser's picture. As he rose and reached for his hat, he tucked it into a pocket. "I'll give it back to you, Gage, but let's show it to Jupp first. Slim, mind the office. I won't be gone long."

He ushered Jim out and conducted him to the Jupp store. En route, had he glanced backward, he might have noted a scruffy, undersized Mex following at a respectful distance. They passed the Western Union office and Jim snapped his fingers and remarked, "I'd best not forget to wire my wife before I leave this town."

"You're married?" prodded Ilford.

"With a son," nodded Jim.

"Gage, I hope your wife's an understanding lady," declared Ilford. "You've left her and your boy to ride the Lord alone knows how far — to square accounts with the lowdowns who killed a horse of yours?"

"She *does* understand," Jim assured him. "I was riding Hank when we first met, and that was a long time ago. We aren't talking about just any saddle-animal. He was special and not only to me. Everybody at my spread, everybody in Cornerstone."

"So now I understand," muttered Ilford. "And now we know Mulhauser'll kill a man as brutally as he'll kill a horse."

When they reached the store, the Jupps were between customers. Jim purchased a few supplies, including tobacco, from Janet Jupp, while Ilford showed her husband the picture. But for her presence, Jupp would have used harder language to vent his spleen on the subject of the photograph.

"He was bandanna-masked like the other two polecats, Sheriff," he said bitterly, and felt at the lump on his forehead. "But this is his picture sure enough. Those eyes! Damn him, he'd have to be the most dangerous madman . . . !"

"No question about that," sighed Ilford, returning the picture to Jim. "This kind of madman, though his brain's twisted, can be cunning as a fox. I guess I don't have to warn you to keep that in mind, Gage, while you're bird-dogging him."

"I'm not about to take chances," said Jim. After they quit the store, he asked about an old acquaintance. "This friend of mine they tangled with at the homestead could be resting here. One of them managed to crease him. Has he been seen?" He offered a good description of the irascible dude he remembered as clearly as he remembered a couple of nomadic Texans. "A sporting man with expensive tastes. He'd most likely check into your finest hotel."

"I haven't noticed a stranger answering that description — which doesn't mean he couldn't be here," shrugged Ilford. "Look around. You've only just arrived, but you only need to use your eyes to realize this is no small town. If my deputies and I could keep track of every new face shows up in Sawyerville, it'd be a miracle."

"I might go look for him after I rent a room," said Jim.

"Fine," nodded Ilford. "Now, in case this is the last I'll see of you, I'd better feed you a little information that'll help with your search. The men you're huntin' tried to steal a horse at the homestead, you said."

"Beaumont's bay. One of 'em complained his mount had colic."

"It all fits, Gage. A colicky horse was left at Walter's livery stable where they broke the hostler's skull. The animal they took as a replacement was Lee Walter's own saddler, a strawberry roan."

"All right, I'll remember that."

"Remember this too. As well as grabbing Jupp's cash and a lot of provisions, one of Mulhauser's cronies, the blond one, helped himself to a new hat, a pearl-grey Stetson."

"I'll keep that in mind too."

"And, when you pick up their tracks again, remember one set of hoofprints'll be different. That'll be the strawberry roan."

"Thanks for your help," Jim said as they shook hands.

Ilford started back to his office and, while Jim was on his way to the Sutton barn, Benito caught up with him.

"Where we go now, amigo?" he demanded.

"We collect our gear and check into a hotel — if you still plan on travelling along with me," said Jim.

"Where you go, amigo Jim, I go," Benito earnestly assured him.

"But you'll disappear the moment we run into danger," predicted Jim.

"No!" protested Benito. "I will be brave!"

"And I'll become president of the United States," jibed Jim.

From the livery stable, after collecting their personal effects, they sought a hotel. Fate being fickle, Jim's choice was the Duffield, where the desk clerk eyed his small companion askance. Jim deemed it politic to assure him that, if Benito misbehaved to eject him from the premises. *He* would see to that chore, and use his boot.

"Two singles, and they don't have to be side by side, or even on the same floor," he told the clerk, as he inked the pen to sign the register.

Then he paused with the pen poised, his eyes on the signatures of the last two transients to check in here. For the first time since Hank's death, he felt like grinning, and did.

"Something amusing?" asked the clerk.

"To me, sure," said Jim. "L. Valentine and W. E. Emerson, Room Fifteen?"

"Upstairs," nodded the clerk. "They're in their room right now." He winced and added, "With an Indian, a fat, disreputable looking Indian. I can't say I approved, but they vouched for him, so I was disinclined to protest. Those Texans are so rough — and so tall."

"You don't have to worry about them, nor the Indian," soothed Jim. "Take my word, at this time they'd be three of the best men staying at his hotel. Do you have vacancies up there, a couple of singles?"

"Rooms Twelve and Fourteen are directly opposite Number Fifteen," said the clerk, offering two keys.

Jim and Benito signed the register. He paid for their overnight stay, after which they hefted their gear to the staircase and began climbing. Jim chose Room 12 and handed Benito the other key. They let themselves in, dumped their effects, opened windows and returned to the corridor.

While Benito eyed him curiously, the big man stood by the door numbered 15 and, for a few moments, forgot his personal loss, the death of the great black stallion, the wife and son no doubt missing him and the aggravation of again being dogged by the dissolute little Mex. He knew the men beyond that door, two he could never forget, also that rarest of all half-breeds, knew them well. Their proximity was more than enough to nudge his funny bone and remind him of the other times he had met them, the better times.

"Stand to one side," he quietly ordered Benito. Then he thumped on the door and raised his voice. "Open up in the name of the law!"

There were muttered oaths from inside. Next, Stretch's voice.

"The law?"

"Federal law!" growled Jim. "I'm a United States marshal here to arrest two fakers name of Valentine and Emerson!"

Came Larry's indignant challenge.

"Fakers — *us?*"

"The charge is masquerading as Texans," Jim said threateningly. "Our records prove Valentine was born in Michigan and Emerson in Minnesota! You lowdown liars aren't even southerners, much less Texans!"

"Let me at that door!" snarled Larry.

He turned the knob, swung the door open and gaped. Jim nodded genially and asked, "Something bothering you?"

Larry stopped gaping, grinned a broad grin and greeted him gleefully.

"Jim Gage, you old sonofagun!"

"Larry, you haven't changed a bit," observed Jim.

Slow Wolf, forever preoccupied with protection of his secret, was at first apprehensive when Larry and Jim withdrew into the room, followed by the runty Mex. But then he recognized the big man, another of the few aware of his superior education, and rose to welcome him warmly.

"Friend James, this is an unexpected pleasure."

"Good to see you again, Slow Wolf," smiled Jim, offering his hand.

"Holy Hannah, look who's here — and as hefty as ever!" enthused Stretch. "I'll be doggoned!"

"Howdy there, you beanpole reb," chuckled Jim.

"Can you beat this?" Larry challenged everybody. "Jim's here — with the sawn-off Mex still sneakin' in his shadow."

"Mucho gusto!" leered Benito. "I am so happy you meet me again, amigo Larry, amigo Stretch, amigo Slow Wolf!"

The handshaking and back-patting continued for some thirty seconds after which the inevitable question, 'What the hell're you doing here?' was voiced. The Texans volunteered that, with Slow Wolf, they were planning a little hunting and fishing in the Rockies, then remarked on the obvious fact that Jim was a long way from home.

"Some unfinished business," he told them.

"And how *is* business, may one enquire?" asked Slow Wolf. "You are, as I recall, the owner of a horse ranch."

"Spread's coming along well," said Jim. "We're husband and wife now, May and me. With a son . . . " He crouched and lowered a hand, "about so high."

"Spittin' image of his pappy I bet," grinned Stretch.

"Chip off the old block," guessed Larry.

"Favors his mother a lot," said Jim. "So he's a good-looking boy."

"Well now, you know why we're here," prodded Larry. "What's your excuse? Unfinished business you said?"

"I'm hunting too, but not for game," muttered Jim. "Been trailing three bad ones all the way from my south quarter. They'd be the same three robbed a storekeeper here, killed a stablehand and stole a horse."

"We heard about that," frowned Stretch. "They'd be bad medicine I reckon, but how come you . . . ?"

"Remember Hank?" challenged Jim.

"C'mon, would we forget him?" grinned Larry. "Great horse."

"A truly magnificent black stallion," Slow Wolf wistfully remembered. "Proud of stance. A thoroughbred."

"He'd be quite an age now, but I bet he's still as handsome a critter," remarked Larry.

"I'd retired him to stud," said Jim. "Yes, he was no youngster and he'd earned his rest. He sired some of the best saddle-animals on the spread. His fast-running days were over but, sometimes, I'd ride him into Cornerstone, keep him to an easy pace. He used to enjoy that — his old boss astride him again — and the townfolk never stopped admiring him."

Slow Wolf winced. Benito averted his eyes, while the Texans traded troubled glances.

"Jim," Larry said gently. "Is Hank . . . ?"

"He had to die sometime, but it

should've been peaceful for him," said Jim, fishing out his makings.

He rolled and lit a smoke and talked a while, the Texans and Slow Wolf listening intently. His run-in with three shabby strangers outside the Cornerstone barber shop was described. He recounted all he had learned of an ex-convict named Mulhauser, told of his bird-dogging the three out of Nevada and through the Utah Territory to the Cobb homestead, then to here, ending with the sheriff's assurance that he would pick up the trail again east of Sawyerville. He then showed the newspaper report, which was passed around.

Now Larry read his mind.

"Gunnin' a good horse down was bad enough, but . . . "

"You're way ahead of me," Jim acknowledged. "Well, that's how your brain works, Larry."

"Somebody's got to stop them sonsabitches," Stretch said grimly.

"The stablehand at the barn where

they stole a strawberry roan, they could've left him gagged and hogtied," muttered Larry. "Didn't have to gunwhip him — kill him."

"I have the feeling the storekeeper is lucky to be alive," sighed Slow Wolf.

"They're the kind leaves misery behind of 'em every place they go," scowled Larry.

"That's how I read 'em," nodded Jim. "That's why I have to find 'em."

"Won't be just you and the weasel huntin' 'em," declared Larry. "Not from manana on."

"Hell, no," said Stretch. "We're gonna be ridin' together again, Jim. You, us and the Chief."

"Don't give us no argument, Jim," growled Larry. "That was no way for Hank to go, and we admired him plenty."

"You'd be good company and welcome," said Jim. "But Slow Wolf's suddenly nervous."

"Deeply troubled," Slow Wolf said dolefully. "Apprehensive, and already sensing violence. I am, friend James, never the heroic type . . . ”

“Cobardes live longer,” mumbled Benito.

“Cowards do enjoy a longer life span,” agreed Slow Wolf.

“You call yourself a coward, but I’m a mite sceptical about that,” said Jim, “remembering the last time we all got together.” He wrinkled his brow. “Where was that? Can anybody recall?”

Stretch searched his memory.

“Blade City — Spade City — somethin’ like that.”

“Slade City,” said Larry.

“That was the place,” nodded Stretch.

“Around Fourth of July some time back,” Jim reminisced. “Coincidence, Larry. We first met during Fourth of July celebrations in my hometown, Cornerstone. Ran into Doc Beaumont around that time too.”

“And was Doc sore,” Stretch recalled with a grin. “He already knew you and us, but didn’t want to.”

“He calls us altruists,” mused Jim.

"And the jokes on him. Right when he's claiming he doesn't care a damn about his fellow men, *he* turns altruist."

"Chief," Larry traded stares with the pudgy redman. "You don't *have* to come along. Jim and us cut sign pretty good. On the other hand, you've forgot more about trackin' than we ever learned."

"I am committed," shrugged Slow Wolf. "I'll be a nervous ally, my friends, but an ally just the same."

"Speaking of Doc, I forgot to mention he's probably here in Sawyerville," offered Jim. "He's the one fazed off Mulhauser and his buddies from the Cobb homestead. A slug creased him. He treated his own wound — isn't that typical?" With a wry grin, he added, "He also delivered the Cobb's first grandchild. You can imagine how he enjoyed *that*."

"He's here, Jim," said Larry. "We saw him, but he didn't see us. Knew he was wounded too. The Chief did a little spyin' on him."

Jim got to his feet.

"You're my supper guests — I insist," he announced. "I have to wire May, but then I'll join you in the dining-room here. After that . . . " He stroked his strong jaw, "we ought to check on Doc you know. We'll be quitting this town tomorrow morning and, if only for old time's sake — what do you say?"

"Sure," shrugged Stretch. "Ain't as if he'll be hard to find. Fanciest saloon in town, betcha life."

The big man walked alone to the telegraph office, Benito choosing to stay and socialize with old acquaintances, one of whom, the only one owning a watch, gave him fair warning. The Valentine boot would kick him clear across Main Street if the Valentine timepiece or the Valentine wallet tempted a certain larcenous Mex to get up to his old tricks.

The telegrapher, remarked, "This is no short message."

"I can afford the charge," Jim assured

him. “Don’t believe I could cut it any shorter, but read it back to me anyway.”

The Western Union man obliged.

‘Mrs J. C. Gage, care of Western Union, Cornerstone, Nevada. Search proceeds. Have company now. Larry, Stretch, Slow Wolf, Benito. Like old times. Love, Jim.’

He suggested, “If we leave out ‘like old times’ . . .”

“No, send it as it reads,” ordered Jim, producing his wallet. “‘Like old times’ will have special meaning for my wife.”

He returned to the Duffield Hotel and a congenial supper with trusty companeros. After that meal, having been informed by the desk clerk that Butler’s Casino was the finest saloon in town, they visited that handsome establishment.

Sawyerville was quiet this evening. Reasoning that robbery and murder were rare occurrences nowadays, and remembering his deputies’ hectic activity of the past twenty-four hours, Sheriff Ilford had decided there'd be no necessity for patrol duty. It couldn't happen two nights in a row; lightning doesn't strike in the same place twice.

Or so he believed.

So Slim Moore and Curly Fuller were taking their ease on a sidewalk bench when, in the bright light of Main Street's lamps, they saw the five men approaching the casino.

"How d'you like that for a mixed bunch?" grinned Fuller.

"Mixed is putting it mild," Moore observed. "Three tough-looking whites, a Mex and an Injun. A *real* mix."

"The three big hombres're going in," noted Fuller. "The Mex and the Injun're gonna hang around out front, looks like."

"I'm still hoping for a quiet night," shrugged Moore. "Never any trouble at Butler's. Best regulated saloon in town."

When Jim and the Texans entered,

one of Butler's tablemen was on duty at the roulette layout. The lady known as Eve would take over from him fifteen minutes from now. She was trading talk with a barkeep when, failing to spot the man they sought at any of the poker tables, the newcomers bellied up to the bar.

Larry ordered three shots of rye. The barkeep performed while Stretch put the question.

"New sportin' gent in town. Good-lookin' and a real dude six foot tall. Name of Beaumont. Any feller like that been here tonight?"

"Don't sound familiar to me," said the barkeep.

"We'll keep looking," Jim said as they raised their glasses. "Can you think of a toast, Larry?"

"Good huntin'," Larry said bluntly.

"I'll certainly drink to that," declared Jim.

Eve watched them down their whiskey; it was her turn to put a question.

"This gent you're looking for, he

craves high stake poker?"

"All the time," said Jim, touching his hatbrim to her. "I was told this place was his destination. He hoped to find three high rollers here."

"Merrill Peters and two of his kind, sure," she nodded. "He'd have to be the gambler you're speaking off. Good manners, knows how to treat a lady?"

"That's him," said Larry. "So he *was* here?"

"Not for long," she said. "You're right. Handsome feller, though he was looking a little peaked."

"*Got* to be him," opined Stretch.

"Big disappointment for him," she offered. "I had to tell him those big shots left on the morning stage. He just missed them."

"Any notion where we'd find him?" asked Larry.

"I steered him to Miller's Alhambra," she recalled. "He wanted to know the best hotel in town, and that's it."

They thanked her and were about to leave when she remembered something else.

"If he's not at the hotel, there's another place you might find him."

"You're being mighty helpful," said Jim. "We appreciate it. And just where else do you think he might be?"

"I don't miss much," she confided.

"And that's no lie," grinned the barkeep.

"There's a cheap tinhorn, a sharper name of Pawley Hawke, hangs around here sometimes," Eve told the seekers. "Drums up trade for a hell-house downtown, a gyp joint called the Even Break."

Abruptly, the barkeep stopped grinning.

"That dump," he growled. "Rusty Gus should've closed it down long before now. And to think Herb Conklin's got the gall to give it such a name. Even break my eye."

"Just give Gus Ilford time — and a chance," Eve urged him. "He can't act without evidence. One of these nights, a sore loser bounced by that ape Gruhan will swear a charge. And that's all the law needs."

"Trouble is, after they've been worked over by Gruhan, they're too scared," complained the barkeep.

"The time'll come," she predicted.

"You were about to tell us more about Hawke, this tinhorn," prodded Larry.

"He talked to the gent you're looking for," said Eve. "Five'll get you ten he persuaded him to try his luck at Conklin's. Conklin slips him a few bucks for doing that. Hawke and all the regulars at the Even Break're Conklin's friends. And every new man in town, every stranger gets into a poker party there, he can kiss his bankroll goodbye."

"Conklin's a lousy cheat," the barkeep said in disgust. "And the joint's always full of hangers-on that'll back him up. That's how that fat skunk stays in business."

"Our friend's a pro," frowned Stretch. "As eagle-eyed as my partner here. He can spot a trick play quick as you can wink."

"At a place like the Even Break, that could be unhealthy for him," warned Eve.

"Downtown?" mused Jim.

"Last block south, this side of the street," she said.

"Much obliged," Larry acknowledged.

"Uh huh," grunted Stretch. "To both of you."

Larry dropped money on the bar.

"Whatever the lady's drinkin'," he told the barkeep. "Pour one for yourself too, and keep the change."

Jim and the drifters departed in ill humor and started downtown with the half-breed and the little Mex trotting to keep up with them.

"You know, I hope we don't find Doc there," Stretch said worriedly.

"I know what you mean," nodded Larry. "He's a dude can take care of himself in any kind of ruckus, guns, fists, whatever, but maybe not right now."

"Not with a wound slowing him down," opined Jim. "Damn it, he's only human."

Watching from their vantage-point, the deputies again traded comments.

"If you don't smell something, *I* sure do," declared Moore. "And it's got a name."

"Trouble," guessed Fuller.

"That's the word," said Moore. "Look at 'em."

"I'm looking," Fuller assured him.

"Recognize 'em?" challenged Moore.

"Didn't when I checked on 'em at Duffield's Hotel," said Fuller. "Didn't get time. I was hustling."

"That's nothing new," retorted Moore. "When did you ever move slowly? Well, I can name two of 'em."

"Same two I checked," nodded Fuller. "Valentine and Emerson — and looking plenty sore about something."

"The other big hombre's from Nevada, name of Gage, talked to Gus a while ago," offered Moore. "I'll allow he seems like a reasonable feller."

"I've heard it said Valentine and Emerson're reasonable enough," remarked Fuller.

"Maybe so," said Moore. "But, when they get into a fight, they're inclined to fight in a destructive way."

"Destructive, right, yes," agreed Fuller. "So we ought to tag 'em?"

"Well," said Moore. "We oughtn't just rest our asses on this seat and make believe we never saw those trouble-shooters pass by — looking mean enough to wrestle a couple grizzlies."

Having mutually agreed they should at least keep the Texans under observation, the deputies quit their seat and became cautiously mobile.

Five admirers of Doc Beaumont were now approaching the headquarters of Herb Conklin, saloonkeeper, glutton and card-sharp. The Even Break made no favorable impression on them. It could have used some fixing, some painting, this clapboard gyp joint. The elements had weakened its plank walls; its shingled roof appeared none too secure.

Intimidated, Slow Wolf and Benito elected to remain outside and study the interior through the grimy front window. Jim and the Texans nudged the batwings inward and entered.

And Doc Beaumont was there.

6

'We Can Use The Exercise'

THE barkeep was brawny, the bouncer even more so. The latter, a large character with shaggy hair and piggy eyes, perched on a stool that seemed too flimsy to support his great weight and watched the poker party, sparing only a cursory glance for the three strangers advancing to the bar.

Jim ordered rye, after which he and the Texans propped elbows and half turned to survey the only poker players in the place. The five were seated at a table by the northside wall, one of whom was undoubtedly an old compadre of theirs, looking as dapper as ever. Doc hadn't missed their entrance, but was pretending he didn't know them, and not just because he held heroes in low regard.

By now, it was painfully obvious to him he should have ignored Pawley Hawke's advice. Hawke was in the game. The fat, florid Herb Conklin was dealing. The other players had been introduced to him as Gough and Nixon, both shifty-eyed men whom he realized — so belatedly that it angered him — were as crooked as Conklin and Hawke. Thunderation. He had suffered only a shadow wound in that shoot-out with the would-be horse thieves, but no use fooling himself. Nothing wrong with his brain nor his eyesight, but he was physically weak.

The only other party present, a roughneck of a size with the hefty barkeep, lounged in a chair placed close to the entrance; there was no rear exit.

"Want to sit in on the game?" growled the barkeep. "New blood's always welcome. It'd be okay by the boss."

"Not right now, thanks just the

same," said Larry.

"We're just killin' time," Stretch said casually.

Doc Beaumont bitterly resented what was happening. Being a gentleman gambler, he despised cardsharps as much as Messrs Valentine, Emerson and Gage despised horse thieves. He also resented the intrusion of three rock-fisted acquaintances he regarded as compulsive do-gooders. What he hated most of all, however, was that their surprise arrival had given him an edge on Conklin and his double-dealing cronies. In his present reduced condition, he couldn't afford to accuse Conklin. The accusation would trigger a violent reaction with which he could not cope.

At least that *had* been the situation. Now that those three muscle-bound ex-cavalrymen were on hand, he could rely on their support. He hated that, for it meant he would be indebted to them, which was insufferable. But, most of all, he hated being cheated.

With his eyes on Conklin's pudgy paws, he said scathingly, "You dealt yourself *another* card from under the deck. Third time, Conklin. And your friend Hawke and these other two are as cunning but as clumsy as you, when it comes to cheating."

"Beaumont, you're a sore loser," leered the fat man. "I never yet allowed a sharper in my place of business."

"I told you," Hawke reminded Doc. "Not for nothing is this place named the Even Break."

"I'll thank you not to address me, Hawke," Doc retorted without deigning to glance at him. "You're no better than what the British call a tout. If this were a whore-house, you'd undoubtedly be Conklin's pimp."

"Now, Beaumont, that's mighty unfriendly talk," chided Conklin, still leering.

"I won't bandy words with you," snapped Doc. "I'm down five hundred dollars. In an honest game, that wouldn't bother me. But I'll allow no man to cheat me. So I'll take my five hundred from the pot and leave."

"The hell you will," muttered Conklin. "Don't try reaching for that fancy pistol of yours — or the pot. One thing you got right. You're sure as hell leaving, but the hard way. Gruhan, throw him out."

The bouncer's eager grin boded ill for Doc, but was quickly erased by Larry's growled command.

"Don't budge from that stool!"

Doc grimaced. Conklin and his cronies switched their attention to the three strangers whose glasses were empty and back on the bar, who stood facing the poker table, Larry closest the bar.

The barkeep made to reach under the counter. Larry caught that movement from the side of an eye and, doubting he would grope for a bar-wiper, a spare handkerchief or a half-smoked cigar, swung a backhander that sent him lurching to the shelves. He struck them hard, glaring with blood trickling from the side of his mouth, and dislodged glassware and bottles that fell and shattered.

Hawke's hand darted under his coat — and stayed there. The sharpers froze to the clicking sounds of four six-shooters cocking. The Colts had cleared leather at eye-defying speed, Larry's, both of his partner's and Jim's long-barrelled Cavalry model.

"Let's see your paw, feller," Stretch ordered the bug-eyed Hawke. "And it better come out empty, else you're pigmeat."

Hawke let go of his armpit-holstered pistol to reveal an empty hand. Conklin, Gruhan and the others were narrow-eyed and watching the four levelled Colts, when Jim addressed Doc.

"We know about your wound, so no arguments. Time for you to go, Doc. Pick up the cash they cheated you of and get out of here."

"Damn and blast you do-gooders," grouched Doc. But he gathered up his cash, stowed it in his wallet and got to his feet. "How I hate being obligated to you!"

With a last contemptuous glance at Conklin and Company, he turned and made for the entrance. The man lounging there decided to play the bravado and defy Doc's rescuers, rose and side-stepped to the doorway to block his exit. He grinned challengingly and bunched his fists. Doc kept coming, eyed him in exasperation and, for a moment, forgot his wound. His left boot swung straight to the man's right shin, causing him to howl and hop. He clobbered the human obstruction with a roundhouse right, driving him to the floor, then stepped over him, out the doorway and onto the sidewalk.

"Psstt!" Benito hissed at him.

He winced in exasperation and moved along to join the little Mex and the pudgy half-breed by the street window. He was no happier to see them than he was Jim and the Texans. The deputies were arriving; he ignored them.

Conklin was seething now. For the first time, a pigeon had gotten away from him before he could pluck him clean; he hungered to square accounts with the rescuers.

"Pretty slick," he taunted. "Only reason you heroes pulled guns — you're too yellow to stand up to Gruhan."

Larry, Stretch and Jim promptly uncocked and reholstered their pistols. Gruhan's eyes lit up. He chuckled harshly and rose from his stool. Conklin, Hawke, Gough and Nixon were suddenly on their feet, their demeanor distinctly warlike.

"Want to think twice about this?" Larry offered. "You try beatin' up on us, we'll defend ourselves. Better believe that."

"We can use the exercise," warned Jim.

The warnings fell on deaf ears. The sharpers charged with the bouncer leading the rush and the barkeep moved again, but not fast enough to be unnoticed by Larry, who whirled and vaulted the bar to grab at him just as he seized a sawn-off shotgun.

Doc, Slow Wolf and Benito were suddenly aware they were being joined at the window by the deputies. Frowning at them, Doc voiced a challenge.

"As officers of the law, it's your duty to put a stop to this."

"Right, yes," nodded Fuller.

"But no hurry," decided Moore. "We figure Valentine and Emerson and the big feller'll damage this hell-house."

"As well as Conklin and his buddies," said Fuller.

"And that'd please Rusty Gus a whole lot," explained Moore.

The first hostile to reach Jim was Nixon, who was brandishing a knife. He slashed at the big man, who backstepped, then captured his right wrist and twisted mercilessly. Nixon wailed, the knife clattered to the floor and then Jim spun him round and landed a powerful kick to his backside. Nixon hurtled across the bar-room and struck the side wall with such impact that sun-dried planks gave way; he disappeared through a jagged opening.

"Now *that's* what I call *damage*," enthused Fuller.

"This ruckus has possibilities," remarked Moore.

While Hawke and Gough threw themselves at Jim, while Larry and the burly barkeep grappled for possession of the shotgun, Stretch braced himself to deal with the massive Gruhan. Urged on by the fat man, the giant lumbered at the taller Texan with his arms spread, telegraphing his intentions.

Stretch knew what to expect, if he let it happen — the bouncer seizing him in a bear-hug, crushing him, breaking ribs. When Gruhan was within striking distance, he thwarted him by slamming three hard ones to his belly. That stopped Gruhan in his tracks. He was wheezing when Stretch unwound a mighty uppercut with devastating accuracy. The bouncer reeled wildly, knocking a pillar loose on his way to the poker table; he slumped on it and it collasped under his formidable weight. The pillar toppled, Conklin dodged it as it fell, and a section of the roof sagged.

Behind the bar, the barkeep had managed to cock both barrels of the shotgun, but Larry was still giving him a bad time. When one barrel discharged, the weapon had been forced backward. The blast of buckshot demolished just about everything on the rear shelves, bottles, glassware, also the back bar mirror. Larry freed his left hand, made a fist and pounded his adversary's ribs, simultaneously forcing the muzzles upward. Another blast. The second barrel discharged to inflict further damage in the ceiling; roof shingles slid down through the hole. And then Larry, eager to get at Conklin, broke the barkeep's grip, seized him by his hair and slammed his head on the bartop face-first. He did that twice, let the out-cold barkeep flop to the floor and, for the second time, vaulted the bar.

All Gough and Hawke achieved by trying to grapple with Jim was a lot of pain — to themselves. He was discouraging them with his left elbow and his jabbing, punishing right fist. Hawke broke loose to get behind him but, before he could pin Jim's arms, Jim lunged forward. His bunched left exploded in Gough's face and, in his staggering backward journey to a corner, Gough wrecked two chairs and overturned another table.

Whirling, Jim took a punch from Hawke, grinned mirthlessly and grabbed him by pants-belt and an arm and lifted him off his feet. He carried his struggling burden six feet toward the entrance before hurling him; Hawke knocked a batwing door from its corroded hinges on his way to the sidewalk, which he hit with a resounding thud.

Nixon had climbed back in and was about to rush Stretch when Larry intercepted him. A hard left loosened Nixon's teeth, a harder right to the midriff doubled him. Relentlessly, Larry grabbed him by his collar, turned him toward the bar and ran at it, taking him with him. When he let go, Nixon's head and shoulders smashed its timber front.

The man clobbered by Doc was upright again. With a chair raised high, he charged at Jim; some brawlers just don't know when to quit. Ducking, Jim felt the chair swish over his head and, from his bent position, gave his attacker the old one-two, a hard belly punch followed by a bone-breaking right to the face. At speed, the man travelled backwards.

"Get clear!" warned Moore.

The deputies, Doc, Slow Wolf and Benito hastily vacated their viewpoint. Onto the sidewalk crashed Jim's victim in a welter of broken glass.

"Careful, Gage, confound you!" fumed Doc, while the ever-obliging Slow Wolf plucked slivers of glass from his frock-coat.

"This could do it," Moore cheerfully predicted.

“Right, yes,” agreed Fuller.“Got to hand it to those trouble-shooters and the big feller. They do great work.”

Gruhan had caught his wind and risen from the wreckage of a table. His teeth were bared. He was clutching the neck of a broken bottle when he rushed Larry, who saw murder in his piggy eyes. He sidestepped as the bouncer swung at him, moved in close and threw his right to the jaw, but his aim was off. His fist struck the giant’s Adams apple.

Watching Gruhan freeze with his eyes glazing, Larry called to Jim.

“If you ain’t too busy . . . ”

“I guess it’ll take the both of us,” Jim said as he approached. “We aren’t as young as we used to be.”

“Yeah, well, before we get any older . . . ” suggested Larry.

He took Gruhan by his armpits, Jim got a grip on his legs and, staggering under his weight, they toted him to the southside wall.

“On three?” asked Jim.

"On three," nodded Larry. "One — two — *three*."

Viewing this feat from the now glassless street window, the onlookers were profoundly impressed. Like a sack of grain, the bouncer was hurled, and to destructive effect. A third of the plank wall succumbed to the impact of Gruhan's weight; he took smashed planks with him as he pitched into the side alley, leaving a jagged gap that caused the fat man to curse obscenely.

Larry and Jim were mentally debating which of them should take care of Conklin when Stretch took the initiative. As he advanced, the fat man panicked and began hurling missiles at him, anything he could reach, bottles, a spittoon, a portion of a smashed chair, but in vain. Only the spittoon struck Stretch, bouncing off his left shoulder, causing him little or no pain.

With Stretch looming before him, Conklin rashly drew a pistol, but wasn't given time to cock it. Clamping both hands over his fat right forearm, Stretch hauled him to the end of the much the worse for wear bar and pounded at its edge with his wrist. Conklin couldn't take the pain. He let go of the pistol and began raising his other arm to protect himself, but too late. With savage blows, Stretch blackened his eyes, flattened his nose and pummelled his paunch till he was gibbering for mercy, whimpering, flopping to his knees.

Stretch stepped clear, blew on his knuckles and took stock. Side by side in the centre of the floor, Larry and Jim were building cigarettes; they too were surveying the damage.

Shambles was a better word.

The bar sagged drunkenly. One man was unconscious behind it. Only the lower half of the senseless Nixon was visible. His head and most of his torso were still thrust through the hole in the surface of the bar. Gough slumbered in a corner. Hawke and another man were sprawled out front on a sidewalk littered with broken glass, the bouncer out cold in the south alley, Conklin down, spitting blood and still whimpering.

Intermittently, roof shingles were slipping through the hole in the ceiling and thudding to the bar-room floor, a monotonous sound. Not a stick of furniture was intact. The bar and everything behind it had suffered extensive damage. Two walls were holed, a timber support no longer perpendicular, only half of a batwing door still dangled and the victors were being stared at from the shattered street window by three close acquaintances and two lawmen they hoped would not ask foolish questions.

Deputy Moore did offer a suggestion, and most cordially.

"Better come on out before the whole place collapses. I don't know what's keeping the roof on."

"Well, I guess there ain't nothin' more we can do here, runt," remarked Stretch.

"Don't seem like it," shrugged Larry.

"In this situation," Jim said poker-faced, "there's a limit to how much we could hope to accomplish."

They trudged through the wreckage to join the non-prone men out front, two of whom surprised them.

"We won't need a statement from you," Fuller assured them, pocketing a notebook. "Mister Beaumont explained everything and I had him put his name to what I wrote down."

"Sheriff'll rule that's as good as a formal charge," said Moore.

"Sheriff won't be mad at us?" frowned Stretch.

"Grateful is what he'll be," grinned Moore. "Besides, you had a right to defend yourselves. You were under attack. We saw everything that happened."

"Didn't occur to you we might need a little help in there?" challenged Jim.

"No," Moore and Fuller said together.

"You takin' them sharpers in?" asked Larry, jerking a thumb.

"Well, certainly," said Moore. "But

no hurry. They'll still be here when we come back for them, too beat to walk, much less make a run for it. Meanwhile, Deputy Moore and I have to find Rusty Gus."

"Who?" frowned Larry.

"Our boss, the sheriff," offered Fuller. "We can't wait to tell him the good news. Let's go, Slim."

"Still a few of 'em inside," Larry reminded the deputies as they began moving away. "This dump could fall down any minute."

"Right, yes," Fuller called over his shoulder. "Any minute."

The victors eyed the grim-faced New Orleans man.

"Well now, Doc," grinned Larry. "No booze left in there, and I figure you owe us . . . "

"My thanks and a drink," Doc acknowledged through clenched teeth.

"You don't have to get sore about it," chided Stretch.

"Yes, I do," retorted Doc. "To be obligated to you drifting roughnecks

— damn you, Gage, why aren't you midwifing mares back where you belong?"

"Well . . . " began Jim.

"You, Slow Wolf, are the exception of course," Doc said courteously. "I give you credit for the speech and manners of a gentleman."

"Very kind of you, friend Vincent," said Slow Wolf.

"As for you — you pernicious parasite . . . " Doc scared hell out of Benito by grasping him by an ear. "Return my watch! Do you imagine I'm unaware you purloined it? As a sneak-thief, you're no smarter than those blackguardly cardsharps!"

"You'll never change, cucaracha," scowled Jim, as the little man surrendered Doc's timepiece.

"I'll kick his ass later," offered Larry. "Right now I'm thirsty."

"So be it," sighed Doc. "We'll repair to my hotel suite."

As they began walking to Sawyerville's finest hotel, Jim gently reprimanded the poker-happy medico.

"I know about that gunplay at the Cobb homestead, and *you* ought to know better than to take chances with a fresh wound."

"You got no patience, Doc," complained Stretch. "One of us could've taken care of that bum 'tween you and the door."

"He was impeding my progress," snapped Doc. "He was an irritation."

"You clobbered him good," Larry recalled. "Think you opened your wound?"

"I may have," shrugged Doc. "Ask me again when we have privacy."

When he led his companions into the luxurious lobby of the Alhambra, the night clerk studied Benito and Slow Wolf in shock. Doc requested his key and demanded that coffee, a bottle of the hotel's best bourbon and extra glasses be delivered to his suite.

"We don't permit Indians . . ." began the clerk.

Then he recoiled in alarm. Larry had

placed both hands on the reception desk and was scowling at him.

"*What* Injun?" he challenged.

"We don't see no Injuns here," drawled Stretch.

"Not a redskin in sight," Jim said amiably.

"My key," growled Doc. "And see that my requirements are delivered promptly."

"Yes, Mister Beaumont," mumbled the intimidated clerk.

Five minutes later, the warriors were keeping Doc company in the parlor of his suite, Slow Wolf sipping coffee, Stretch playing barkeep and distributing double shots of bourbon. Doc half-emptied his glass and, waving off offers of help, removed his frockcoat and vest and began stripping to the waist. That done, he seated himself to study the dressing at his left side.

"I don't see no blood," said Stretch, squinting. "Good sign?"

"No damage," decided Doc. "But I should replace the dressing. I'll permit you to assist, Valentine. Kindly fetch the small valise from my bedroom, bottom drawer of the dresser. But first use the bathroom, wash your hands." While Larry was doing that, he glanced at the pudgy redman squatting crosslegged, drinking coffee. "You've been well, Slow Wolf, I trust?"

"Thank you for asking, friend Vincent," said Slow Wolf. "I still endeavour to live quietly. Unfortunately, that's not always possible."

"Not if you insist on cohabiting with disaster prone Texans," Doc said grumpily. Larry rejoined the party. During the changing of the dressing, the wound was carefully inspected. Doc pronounced himself satisfied. He was healing well. A few more square meals and he would be back to his full strength. Now he frowned impatiently at Jim. "Gage, I hate coincidences, and here you are — you, that scruffy little peon, Valentine and Emerson and Slow Wolf, all together again."

"Like old times, huh?" grinned Stretch.

"That's a depressing comment," complained Doc. "Gage, what in blazes are you doing so far from home?"

Jim took a pull at his drink and spoke calmly

"Man-hunting, Doc."

"Damn it, surely your long search for your brother's murderer was enough," protested Doc. He paused to take scissors and adhesive plaster from Larry. "You achieved your purpose, finally ran the killer to ground . . . "

"I'm after the same three hard cases you tangled with at the Cobb place," said Jim.

"I presume then, they're riding horses stolen from your ranch," said Doc.

"Didn't steal any," muttered Jim. "Killed one. Gunned Hank down."

Doc's face clouded over. He finished securing the dressing and, while redonning the upper half of his underwear and his shirt, eyed the big man uncomfortably.

"Hell, Gage, not the black stallion, the handsome animal who served you so well?" Jim nodded grimly. "*Why*, in heaven's name?"

Jim recounted again his clash with the three rogues in Cornerstone, then proffered the report from the North Nevada newspaper. The New Orleans man read it, studied the photograph in disgust and readily recognized the subject.

"We're stickin' with Jim, Doc," said Larry. "Local deputy tagged their tracks to the east county line. They did some thievery and killin' in this town, so . . ."

"Somebody's got to stop 'em," said Stretch. "And Larry and me got nothin' better to do anyway."

"We're all headed out again," announced Larry. "Right after breakfast."

"Blast," scowled Doc.

"*Now* what're you gripin' about?" frowned Stretch.

"I won't enjoy one moment of it,"

grumbled Doc. "What gentleman of my standing would wish to travel with such hard-nosed roughnecks — Slow Wolf being the only exception? I'll resent it every mile of the way, but I have no choice, I'm committed."

"You don't have to . . . " began Jim.

"Of course I have to!" fumed Doc. "I too have a debt to settle with those blackguards! As well as slaying a truly noble thoroughbred, they inflicted an injury upon my person!"

"Upon your person?" prodded a confused Stretch. "You mean they hurt some friend of yours? You always claim you got *no* friend, *want* no friend . . . "

"I am referring to *myself*, you semi-educated oaf," growled Doc. "For that, I demand satisfaction! So I *have* to accompany you!" Abruptly, he regained his composure. "That gunplay in front of the homestead — unfinished business. They creased me, while the most I achieved was to nick the arm of the one who scored on me and shoot the hat off another. And that's not enough. I have that holed hat and intend returning it to its owner — before punishing him."

"You'll know him when we catch up with 'em," Jim assured him. "He'll be wearing a brand-new pearl-grey Stetson. Sheriff Ilford told me."

"No doubt we'll be leaving early," said Doc. "As you, Gage, and these ruffianly drifters were somewhat over-active this evening, I suggest we call it a day. We'll need to be well rested and alert during this hunt."

"Glad to have you along, Doc." Jim set his empty glass down and eased himself from his chair. "As Stretch said, it'll be like old times."

"If *anybody else* says that . . . " scowled Doc.

"Last time we six got together, it was quite a party," Jim recalled. "But we lived to remember it."

"I was terrified," mumbled Slow Wolf, getting to his feet.

"I was not," bragged Benito.

"The hell you weren't," the Texans jibed in unison.

"Sutton's livery, Doc," offered Larry. "That's where we'll be waitin' for you. Don't worry. We won't leave without you."

"Cold comfort," grouched Doc, as his guests began filing out.

At 8.45 next morning, the gambling medico straddled his spritely bay colt and approached Sutton's stable with all his gear secured. The Texans, Slow Wolf, Jim and Benito were ready, sitting their mounts, enjoying their after-breakfast smokes, patiently awaiting him.

"All right," Jim said when Doc joined them. "East from here."

"May the Great Spirit protect us," sighed Slow Wolf.

"C'mon, let's move," urged Larry.

"Here we go again," drawled Stretch.

And the mixed half dozen turned their horses, heeled them and rode out of Sawyerville, moving east to pick up track of three rogues now idling their animals into the main street of a town some distance to the southeast.

* * *

Lockhart was just coming alive, not many locals in evidence.

"You'd better be right," Mulhauser growled at his nephew.

"This Elgart jasper'd better be here."

"He'll be here, Uncle Carl, count on it," grinned Stack, setting his new headgear at a jaunty tilt. "Said he didn't care how long him and his companeros gotta wait for you. Real wild bunch he calls 'em."

"Lootin' and burnin' Santa Paula'll be fun enough for 'em?" prodded Pacey.

"Betcha life," nodded Stack. "And Sam likes banks, any kind, includin' two-bit banks in half-alive towns."

Pacey touched the tear in his right sleeve and Mulhauser at once scowled at him and muttered a warning.

"I got no use for a man can't work his gunarm."

"Told you before, that tinhorn at the homestead scarce nicked me," said Pacey. "How long did I bleed? Just a couple minutes. All healed now. Nothing wrong with my gunhand."

"Prove it," ordered Mulhauser, and Pacey's right hand was suddenly gun-filled, his pistol clearing the holster fast. "All right, good enough."

"Don't fret on my account," said Pacey. "Any shootin' gotta be done, I'll sure do my share." He stared along the quiet street, his eyes narrowing. "It'll go hard for that tinhorn — if I ever run into him again."

"Keep your eyes peeled," urged Mulhauser.

"I'm lookin'," Stack assured him as they travelled the first block. "You can rely on Sam. Whatever he says he'll do, he . . . " He chuckled and pointed. "There he is now!"

The man emerging from a side alley, waving to them, was tall and black-garbed, sallow-complexioned and well-barbered. Girding his lean loins was a concho-studded shellbelt, double-holstered; his matched six-guns sported mother-of-pearl grips.

"A show-off," Mulhauser observed.

"He's okay," insisted Stack. "Won't let you down, you'll see."

They reined up in the centre of the wide and dusty street and Elgart read that as a hint he should join them there; no danger the few locals on the sidewalks would overhear their conversation.

He approached at an easy stroll, nodded to Stack and Pacey and was careful to accord the wild-eyed one respect.

"My pleasure," he offered. "Willy talked a lot about you. Good to see you again, Carl."

"Where're the gunhands you've been roundin' up?" demanded Mulhauser. "And how many of 'em?"

"Camped a ways south, less'n a hundred yards from the trail we'll ride to Santa Paula," replied Elgart. "Seven. All good boys and cravin' a little action. You got any business here or would you as soon I take you to 'em rightaway?"

"We'll get movin' soon as you've saddled up," growled Mulhauser.

"And loaded a pack-mule — but that won't take long," said Elgart. "Supplies, you know? Grub, extra ammunition, booze."

"Hustle," ordered Mulhauser.

A short time later, Milo Gerard, Lockhart's town marshal, watched the four riders quitting the settlement, one leading a pack-mule, and commented to the crony sitting with him by the door of his office, "Now I'm easier of mind."

"You were leery of him." His crony was, like Gerard, whittling. "Stranger in the black duds, two gun packer."

"Been leery of him all the time he hung around here," confided Gerard. "And them three he rode out with, I'm just as leery of them. You notice the scarecrow with the eyes?"

"Everybody got eyes, Milo."

"Not like *him*. By damn, he's a mean one. Full of hate's my guess — and I wouldn't want to be whoever he's hatin'."

It was a few minutes before 11.a.m. when Elgart led his companions east from the trail to reach the box canyon where his seven cronies lounged about a cookfire.

"Any of 'em wanted by the law?" Mulhauser asked him.

"Four of 'em, but a long way from here — Dakota," said Elgart. "Since I organized this bunch, we've been doin' pretty good, hit a couple stagecoaches and an express office. The boys sure had 'emselves a time."

"They'll have a helluva time in Santa Paula," grinned Stack.

"I guarantee that," muttered his uncle. "If puttin' a town to the torch is their idea of fun, they'll sure get their pleasure."

They rode into the box canyon. The

seven gunmen rose and took charge of the horses, off-saddling them and tying them with their own animals. The mule was relieved of part of its load and cooking gear broken out. While the rogue pack fixed lunch, Elgart identified seven tearaways as predatory, as ruthless as Mulhauser could wish for.

"Clark, Addison, Horrocks and Brell, say howdy to Willy's Uncle Carl. And that's Neeves, Orth and Strueby."

"From here on, I'm boss," Mulhauser announced. "You all savvy that?" The gunmen nodded, listening intently, sizing him up. "When we hit Santa Paula, all I want for myself is to see a righteous bastard name of Farwell die in misery. The bank cash and whatever else you want to loot — you're welcome. Have your fun."

"Then we burn the whole shebang, that right?" Scrawny Neeves licked thick lips as he voiced this question.

"When I give the word, you'll grab every can of coal-oil you can find and douse every place — the bank, stores, shacks, *every* place," declared Mulhauser.

"Sounds good, boys?" challenged Elgart.

"Sounds just fine to me," leered the bewhiskered Horrocks. "I always did hanker to burn me a town."

"Ain't much of Santa Paula, but this is gonna be one helluva party," chuckled Stack.

"Soon as we eat, we get movin'," growled Mulhauser.

"You're the boss," Elgart said cheerfully.

Doc Beaumont felt stronger now, physically at least, but his disposition was becoming incendiary. Would Gage and those uncouth trouble-shooters *never* stop reminiscing?

7

Six Southbound

THEY were far east of Sawyer County, travelling verdant terrain and, thanks to Slow Wolf's tracking savvy, tagging their quarry easily. Flanked by the Texans, Jim kept Junior a respectful thirty yards behind the redman. Doc was behind them, too close behind for his liking; their conversation was audible. The little Mex brought up the rear.

"Yes, that was quite a contest first time we met," Jim was agreeing.

"Fourth of July," mused Larry. "And many a long year ago."

"Your hometown, Jimbo," recalled Stretch.

"Cornerstone," nodded Jim. "And don't think I'm not missing it — and the spread. My shooting eye was working just fine that time, but you southern boys were tough competition."

"Then we got mixed into that San Saba ruckus," Larry reminded him. "Doc was with us, up to his ears in it."

"I still remember the last time we all got together," said Jim. "Quite a fracas that was, the Slade City thing."

"How's everything in Cornerstone nowadays?" asked Stretch.

"You wouldn't notice many changes," said Jim. "Ben Courtney's getting on in years, but still our sheriff. I'm pretty sure, when he retires, Rick Dane'll take over from him. Good man, Rick. The Hair Of The Dog is still the most popular saloon in town and I swear Liam Finnigan doesn't look a day older. Oley Tedrow's still mayor and his brother Griff still running the forge . . . "

"Enough!" Doc groaned aloud. "Spare me this sickening, sentimental nostalgia!"

"Same old Doc," Larry remarked.

"Whatsamatter, Doc?" asked Stretch,

glancing backward. "You don't like talk of old times?"

"I'd rather cut my throat," growled Doc.

"Why don't we give him a break?" Jim quietly suggested to Larry. "He'll feel better for a little congenial conversation, but not with us."

"What'd you say, beanpole?" prodded Larry.

"Only one of us talks as educated as Doc is the Chief," said Stretch. "I'll trade places with him, so he can fall back and palaver with Doc a while." He rode forward to join Slow Wolf. "Clear sign, Chief?"

"As you can see, yes," nodded Slow Wolf. He gestured ahead. "Some fifteen minutes from now, we should reach it. You see it?"

"Looks like a signpost," observed Stretch. "Might be we're comin' to a trail. Listen, I'll spell you. Doc's feelin' a mite grouchy . . . "

"The good doctor's natural condition, it would seem," was Slow Wolf's knowing comment.

"Little company might cheer him some," muttered Stretch. "You talk high-falutin' — like him — so how about you ride along with him a while."

"I'll try to engage him in friendly conversation," said Slow Wolf. He slowed his dun's pace, letting the taller Texan take the lead, letting Larry and Jim pass him, then falling in stirrup to stirrup with the New Orleans man. "Less pain now, I trust, friend Vincent?"

"Barely a twinge, thank you," said Doc. "When we make camp tonight, it will be time for me to discard the dressing. The bullet didn't tear a deep crease, quite shallow fortunately. Slow Wolf, how in blazes did Lady Luck throw you together with those Jonahs *this* time?"

"An over-zealous deputy sheriff charged me with theft," sighed Slow Wolf. "Present company excepted, my friend, but it's a sad fact that many whites jump to uncharitable conclusions upon seeing me in possession of an excellent Winchester rifle and riding this fine animal. They were, as you know, gifts from friends Lawrence and Woodville, but white lawmen refuse to take my word for that. So I was being tried as a thief and, thanks be to the Great White Spirit, those generous Texans reached that town at that time, attended the trail and supported my defence. I should add the presiding judge was obviously Texan and kindly disposed to them."

"*You* have befriended *them* in time of need," argued Doc. "You should not consider yourself obligated to them. It's unfair of them to expect you to travel with them."

"My own decision, I assure you," said Slow Wolf. "Until friend James found us in Sawyerville, it was our intention to hunt the high country together."

"Now we're hunting heartless killers," Doc pointed out. "Probably heading into danger. And you're reluctant to expose yourself to danger, as you have every right to be."

"I cannot deny being apprehensive," confided Slow Wolf. "But, like your good self, I respect and admire fine horses. Friend James' black stallion was a proud and loyal animal. For him to have been so brutally slain in the twilight of his years . . . "

"I agree," Doc said softly. "Gage's warrior instincts have caused me considerable irritation, but I have to concede the man knows horses."

"He too was a cavalryman," Slow Wolf reminded him. "Ironic is it not? A reminder of the futility of war. In that lamentable conflict, friend James fought in the Union Army and attained the rank of sergeant. Our Texas friends of course were troopers of the Confederate Cavalry — so they were once enemies, those three brave souls."

"I sometimes wish they still were," sneered Doc. "Their regard for one another is downright maudlin."

"Fate does play strange tricks,"

reflected Slow Wolf. "The war is in the past. I doubt they even discuss it, for now they are friends and the bond is strong, Vincent, a bond of mutual respect." He dropped his gaze to the decrepit felt hat secured to the bay's cantle. "A souvenir?"

"That's it," Doc nodded coldly. "But for the momentary shock of my wound, I'd have put a bullet in the blackguard's brain instead of merely depriving him of his headgear. Well, as I've stated, I intend returning it."

"How great a distance must we pursue these evil whites?" Slow Wolf wondered. "What could be their destination?"

"They may have *no* destination," suggested Doc. "It's entirely possible they're of the breed who just drift at will, leaving havoc wherever they roam. At the homestead, they meant to steal my mount. In Sawyerville, they succeeded, not only stealing a horse, but butchering a stablehand and gunwhipping and robbing a storekeeper. They are devoid of conscience, Slow

Wolf, ruthless, contemptuous of human life. I advise you to bear that in mind when we finally run them to ground. You claim to be squeamish. Perhaps you are, but you're also devoted to your own welfare. Hold to that thought, keep your rifle cocked, take cover and defend yourself."

"I am resigned to that prospect," Slow Wolf glumly assured him.

Up ahead, Stretch had reined in to study the signpost. He stayed mounted as he called to this companions.

"Found a regular trail. Keep a'comin', but Slow Wolf first."

The pudgy half-breed parted company with Doc, rode past Larry and Jim and was second to reach the trail. As he cooled his saddle to read sign, Stretch announced, "There's a town south, Chief. Lockhart it's called. Looks like that's where they're headed, but you best make sure."

"There is no doubt," Slow Wolf reported as the others arrived. "This is a seldom used trail and they are certainly following it southward."

"We just gonna keep on?" asked Stretch. "Must be near high noon. That's what my belly's tellin' me."

"And our animals need spelling," nodded Jim. "How many miles to Lockhart?" Stretch told him. "We could be there mid-afternoon, allowing for the hour we'll take to eat and tend the horses."

"No sense us sittin' winded critters when we find Mulhauser," opined Larry. "If him and his buddies're still there when we make Lockhart."

With Benito bullied into helping collect firewood, Larry and Jim tended the horses and Stretch and Slow Wolf fixing lunch double-quick, they were in fact on the move again in forty-five minutes.

Marshal Gerard and his only aide, the laconic Deputy Duke Cooper, were lazing in caneback chairs outside the law office when the six strangers appeared, their mounts idling, but four of the riders keeping their eyes busy and their hands close to holsters. Grimacing, Gerard complained, "Ain't we never gonna see *sociable* strangers passin' through? First there was that double gunhung jasper in the black duds, then them three hard cases, and now . . ."

"Quite a mixture," Cooper noted. "Three of 'em could be ranchin' men, one 'a sportin' man for sure, and they got an Injun and a Mex with 'em."

Sighting the local lawmen, Jim muttered a suggestion.

"They'd know if Mulhauser's still here. Might save us some time if a couple of us just ask."

"Let's do that," nodded Larry.

He and Jim left Doc and Stretch and the others to ride to the seated badge-toters. Larry, content to leave the talking to Jim, stayed mounted. The big man swung down from the black, moved to the lawmen, both warily rising now, and dug out his wallet.

"We're trailing three riders, the kind

who ought to be locked in your jail," he began.

"I'm Marshal Gerard, this here's Deputy Cooper and we ain't holdin' no prisoners," muttered the boss-badge.

"Three mean-lookin' hombres stopped by, but not for long," offered Cooper.

"He one of 'em?" demanded Jim, proffering the strip of newsprint.

Both lawmen studied the photograph; one look sufficed.

"Him for sure," Gerard declared as he returned the paper. "There was a gunslick hangin' around town for near a week. Plain enough he was waitin' for the jaspers you're interested in. They rode on with him. He's leadin' a pack-mule."

"You get his name?" asked Jim. They shook their heads. "Tell me about him."

He wore no badge, but his demeanor was so authoritative that neither Gerard nor Cooper felt the urge to ask questions; they just answered his.

"Lean feller, dangerous I'd reckon,"

said Gerard. "Rigged all in black 'cept for a fancy gunbelt. Packs a brace of pistols with pearl grips, real purty. And his holsters're tied down — just like yours."

"Which way from here?" frowned Jim.

"South," said Gerard.

"Nearest town south?"

"Only one I know of'd be Santa Paula. It ain't much, just a worked out mine town."

"You get many visitors up from Santa Paula?"

"Never seen none. And Lockhart folks got no call to travel down there."

"So that south trail isn't travelled much," Jim supposed. "Fine. It'll be that much easier to follow their sign. Much obliged, Marshal." As he retreated to Junior, he thought to assure the lawmen, "You can be thankful Mulhauser and his friend's visit was so brief."

"Glad to see 'em move on," said Gerard. "Them and the gunslick. They looked like trouble."

Jim remounted and bluntly assured him, "That's what they are. The worst kind."

The six rode out of Lockhart to follow the south trail again. Track of their quarry, plus a fourth horse and the mule, showed clear; Slow Wolf was spared the duty of riding point. Tersely, Jim repeated his conversation with the lawmen. After that, Stretch was the first to comment.

"Plain enough they picked up a sidekick. And the pack-mule could mean Mulhauser's lookin' to collect more help."

"It'd help if we knew how many," remarked Larry. "And maybe we'll find out."

They found out while there was still ample daylight. Reaching the point at which Elgart had led the trio off the trail, they did likewise. Then they were sitting their mounts at the entrance to the small box canyon, only Larry and Slow Wolf entering afoot to read sign.

While the redman felt at the earth used to smother the fire, Larry prowled around carefully, studying hoofprints. Slow Wolf concurred with his findings. They returned to the canyon mouth and remounted.

"Tracks lead back to the trail," Stretch announced, pointing.

"How many, Slow Wolf?" prodded Jim.

"Mulhauser has been joined by others of his kind," Slow Wolf said uneasily. "I agree with Lawrence's tally. Eleven horsemen in all, and the mule."

"And how much farther must we follow them?" wondered Doc. "Just where *are* they bound — and why?"

"Maybe we never find them," suggested Benito, sounding hopeful.

Jim scowled at him. He shrugged and averted his eyes. "Tracks look fresh," said Stretch.

"Uh huh," grunted Larry. "So we go careful from now on."

"Damn right," nodded Jim. "It

mightn't have crossed Mulhauser's mind that I'd chase him clear across Nevada and Utah, but his sidekicks could have a drag rider watching their back-trail."

"Everybody stay sharp," Larry urged, as they started back to the trail.

They pushed south warily that afternoon, Slow Wolf in the lead and intently watching the terrain ahead, alert for his first glimpse of a rear scout. To the east, the hunters had a view of the soaring snow-capped peaks of the Rocky Mountains, to the west open country broken by rockmounds and a variety of vegetation, spruce, mahogany, quaking aspen. No sign their quarry had quit the trail, so what lay ahead?

"That wild-eyed bastard didn't recruit eight extra guns for no reason," Jim opined to Doc and the Texans.

"If he had dinero stashed for instance, the left-over loot from some job he pulled before he went to prison," reasoned Stretch, "he wouldn't be lookin' to share it with eight other hombres."

"Let's not try to read his mind," muttered Doc. "I call that futile — considering we're dealing with a madman."

"He has more pistoleros now," winced Benito. "And we are only six."

"More like five and a half," Doc said caustically.

"Relax, short-ass," said Larry. "If we have to take all eleven of 'em, that's what we'll do."

Toward evening, Jim began scanning the boulder-littered rises left of their route. He voiced a possibility already being considered by the trouble-shooters.

"Raiding their nightcamp wouldn't be a brilliant tactic, not by any means. We've tagged them a good distance, but Mulhauser could still be a lot of miles from his destination, so they *could* nightcamp."

"Means *we'll* need to hole up someplace," nodded Larry.

"Well-sheltered," said Doc.

"Yup," grunted Stretch. "No cookfire for us. Dead giveaway."

"When we take 'em, it has to be by surprise and in daylight," insisted Jim.

"Santa Paula you're thinkin'?" prodded Larry. "I heard what them Lockhart badge-toters told you. Don't seem there'd be rich pickin's in a worked out minetown for the whole bunch of 'em, but maybe Mulhauser's got his reasons."

"And we aren't sure how far south that place is," said Doc. "So, if they decide against travelling all night . . . "

"They'll make camp," nodded Jim. "We'd best find a wind-break while there's still daylight." He turned in his saddle to growl at the jittery Benito. "Make yourself useful, cucaracha. Check those low hills ahead and east of us, find a place we can shelter overnight."

The little Mex headed in that direction. Larry rode forward to join Slow Wolf and give instructions. At his first sight of firelight, he was to rejoin the party.

"You'll find us easily enough, Chief."

"I will smell my way to you," Slow Wolf assured him.

It was almost full dark, the Texan's scanning of the sky telling them there'd be little moonlight this night, when Jim and Doc heard Benito's echoing cry of alarm and gave thanks the wind was blowing from the south.

The hunters detoured off the trail and, a few moments later, spotted the dejected looking roan standing riderless on a flat-topped rise. Larry rode up there, then turned and called to his cohorts.

"Looks like the little feller dropped through a hole. I'll fetch his critter down. You move around to the south side. If we're lucky, he's found us a cave — the hard way."

This proved half-true. What Benito had discovered after dismounting was an abandoned claim. The earth atop the rise had given way under him, depositing him on a pile of it in the hollowed out section into which Stretch and the others now led their horses. Those prospectors of long ago hadn't bored and shored a tunnel. They had hacked directly into the hillside, so this was a man-made cavern. The hole up top might cause a draft, but at least they'd be under cover, ample shelter for horses as well as men.

To Benito's disgruntlement, nobody paid much attention to him. He complained he had suffered a terrifying experience and was in dire agony, but Doc's examination revealed he had only a bruise or two, no broken bones. When they had off-saddled, fed and watered the horses, Doc squatted on his gear, gazed about and remarked, "I wonder if they won anything for their back-breaking efforts, the fools who toiled here. Look at those walls, the marks made by pickaxes."

"Maybe they did hit a pay-vein, Doc," shrugged Jim. "We'll never know."

Confident Slow Wolf would establish the opposition's position undetected, they broke out provisions for a cold supper. They were ready to eat when the redman rejoined them, leading his dun in and off-saddling it, tying it with the other animals.

"It is fortunate you found shelter," he declared. "But even more fortunate that you have made no fire."

"The glow of it . . . " began Jim.

"Exactly," nodded Slow Wolf. "For their night-camp, they detoured to the spine of a high ridge. I saw their fire and, from so high a vantage-point, their lookout would undoubtedly perceive the glow of *our* fire, were we careless enough to build one."

"So we're gettin' close?" asked Stretch.

"I estimate the ridge to be two-thirds of a mile southwest of us," said Slow Wolf.

During that cold meal, Larry waxed curious.

"Supposin' now they *are* makin' for Santa Paula. This Mulhauser's a wild one, no question of that, but wouldn't he have a reason? I mean he's got to be plannin' *somethin'*."

Jim downed a mouthful of cold beans and pork and offered a theory.

"Vengeance could be his purpose. He's a hater and addle-brained. To such men, vengeance isn't just important. It's an obsession. Out of spite, crazed by his need to punish me, he killed a great animal. It's possible, while Ben Courtney was holding Mulhauser and his friends in the Cornerstone jail, they learned about Hank and how much he meant to me. So, to cause me pain, he . . . "

"He'll pay for it, Jimbo," Stretch said gently.

"Muy malo," shuddered Benito.

"You're probably right, Gage," frowned Doc. "If a dying town is his destination, who is his intended victim? Interesting question."

"So maybe he's gunnin' for some hombre, maybe more'n one hombre," muttered Larry.

"When them hard cases reach Santa

Paula . . . " began Stretch.

"Uh huh," nodded Larry. "We better be close behind of 'em, close enough to block Mulhauser from butcherin' some other poor sonofagun, like the stablehand at Sawyerville."

Supper over, they took turns to sit guard in the cave entrance. By sunrise, men and horses were well rested and eager to move on, five of them anyway. Slow Wolf made a forward scout while the other hunters rejoined the south trail.

He was waiting for them almost a mile on, sitting the dun and gesturing to the ridge.

"They broke camp," he reported when they caught up. "They proceed southward. May I advise greater caution now, my friends?"

"We're not all that far behind 'em?" challenged Larry.

"I estimate less than an hour," winced Slow Wolf.

"So," said Jim. "Easy does it."

As they nudged their mounts to

movement again, Benito made no secret of his disquiet.

"So many of these bad hombres."

"Quit your frettin'," Larry chided him. "What do we care if we're outnumbered?"

"Hell, Larry and me're used to it," shrugged Stretch.

"We have an edge," Doc said calmly. "Please — I beg you — do not interpret my remarks as a compliment. But, when it comes to fast and accurate gunplay, I acknowledge you, Valentine and Gage to be my equals. Something you must have learned, having fought so many outlaws, no doubt for want of something better to do, is that all outlaws aren't necessarily expert pistoleros. Some are. Many are not."

"True enough," agreed Jim.

"My apologies for reopening an old wound, Gage," said Doc, "but it must have occured to you that mortally wounding a defenceless horse with rifle-fire did not call for superior marksmanship."

"They got close," Jim said bitterly.

"I anticipate most of this battle will be fought with handguns," Doc continued. "Close range or perhaps not so close range. Under such conditions, speed will not be as vital as accuracy. We must acknowledge Bat Masterson as an authority on this subject, so let's not forget his statement, which is on record. Masterson is sceptical about fast draw gunplay. He insists the victor, the survivor, will always be the combatant whose nerve and aim are steadiest. We'd do well to keep that in mind whether we have to challenge these rogues on open ground or within the confines of a township."

"You're tellin' it true, Doc," drawled Larry.

"Yup," nodded Stretch. "Ain't none of us'd give you an argument."

This day passed like the preceding day, the pursuers going to pains to avoid being sighted by their quarry. Coming upon the hard cases' abandoned nooncamp, they found more than empty food cans; quite a few empty bottles. More of the same when, after another nightcamp with no fire, they investigated the basin in which Mulhauser and Company had spent the hours of darkness. More empty bottles.

"Some of 'em're puttin' it away like water," Larry commented as they moved on. "Might be they've drunk all the booze the mule was totin'. If Santa Paula's where they're headed, the saloon's where they'll likely be. Time they get there, they'll be dry-mouthed again."

* * *

Toward noon of this day, from the front window of the Santa Paula branch of the Trans-National Banking Company, the aging manager, Reavis Farwell, stared uptown and studied the strangers now arriving. Many years had passed. He was slower of movement nowadays, but his sight was keen. He recognized and at once remembered the lead rider. Dear Lord, how could he forget *that* one?

He groaned aloud as he secured the street door and glanced to the stairs leading up to his daughter's living quarters. Davinia! She must leave. He was in no doubt as to why Mulhauser had run him to ground. Already, he considered himself a doomed man. But why should she — and the whole town — fall victim to these marauders? He heard her humming, heard her footsteps, then she was descending the stairs, flashing him the smile that so reminded him of his late wife.

Davinia Farwell was twenty and beautiful, dark-haired, five feet two inches tall and slim-figured.

"Lunch soon," she said cheerily. "And, after lunch, I'll take flowers to Mother's grave."

"Not today, child," he said urgently, moving to her, grasping her shoulders. "Forget lunch. You must do exactly as I tell you — and quickly!"

"You're trembling," she frowned. "What is it?"

He forced himself to phrase his explanation, to express his fears succinctly; precious time would be lost were he made to repeat himself. The arrival of a vengeance-crazed ex-convict and ten heavily-armed men could only mean disaster for this small town he still believed could grow again. That had always been his conviction. There would be another strike, another boom period; Santa Paula would be reborn.

"It can't be coincidence," he declared. "He means to avenge himself, my dear. But for my speech from the witness box, his sentence may have been lighter. But, with so many gunmen backing him, he won't stop with me. Others will be in danger, the people, the whole town. I want you out of Santa Paula as quickly as possible. I couldn't bear for . . . "

"If you think I'd desert you . . . " she began.

"You won't be deserting the town in time of need, you'll be seeking help," he declared. "Your filly is the fastest saddle animal in Santa Paula, so it has to be you who rides to the northeast to Perdido."

"All the way to Perdido?" she gasped.

"How much protection can this town expect from its only law officer?" he challenged. "Luke Deitz is lazy and incapable. But I'm sure the sheriff of Perdido will come to our aid. He'll deputize a force of volunteers when you tell him Carl Mulhauser has brought ten gunmen here."

"I understand now why you've been so uneasy," she murmured. "First a traveller left a newspaper. You read something that unnerved you. Then a stranger arrived . . . "

"Scouting for Mulhauser I'm sure," he nodded. "Please, Davinia, no more talk, no more arguments. Go upstairs and change — into some of my clothes."

"But . . . "

"You mustn't let that fiend see you!

If he does, you'll need to be disguised! From a distance, if you hide your hair under one of my hats, you could be mistaken for a boy. Then you must saddle the filly and creep out of town. Stay clear of Main Street. Work your way west of the slag heaps, walk all the cover you can find."

"I'm so concerned for you."

"And I for you! That's why you have to obey my orders! *Lead* the filly. Don't mount, don't begin riding until you're too far north for them to hear. Hurry now — please!"

The girl hustled upstairs. He returned to the window in time to see the invaders dismount in front of the town's only surviving saloon, the Lucky Lode. When they entered, he began praying they would stay in there long enough for his daughter to make good her escape.

Moments later she was descending the stairs. He had shrunk, lost weight with age. The jacket hung loosely even so. She had tucked the pants into her riding boots and her hair was upswept and secured by a felt hat. Hastily, he unlocked the street door; the building had no rear exit. She kissed him, clung to him briefly, then slipped out and around the south corner to hurry to the back yard.

In the barn, she saddled her chestnut filly. That done, she led the animal out of the yard by its rein and made for the concealment of the debris west of town, the ugly legacy of Santa Paula's boom period, mounds of slag, high heaps of earth and rubbled and rotting timbers.

So much of Santa Paula was in decay, she was thinking as she maneuvered to the west side of the debris. The town's buildings, so many of them constructed of frame and clapboard, were weakened by the heat of summer and the heavy rains of winter.

It would be so easy for her father's enemy to destroy the town he had vowed never to leave.

A safe enough distance north, she

mounted and heeled the filly to a run, while, in the Lucky Lode, the proprietor dared request payment for the whiskey being swigged by eleven fearsome strangers. Brell chuckled harshly and backhanded him. He recoiled, face smarting, nose bloody.

"Did we forget to mention?" jeered Horrocks. "The drinks're on you."

The only locals in the bar-room at this time, two old fossickers, were too intimidated to hang around. They trudged out, passing Mulhauser, who lounged by the batwings, enjoying their fear and the fear of all Santa Paula folk who had witnessed his arrival. Soon enough, he would put his recruits to work. Meanwhile, let them fire themselves up. And let Reavis Farwell sweat it out in any agony of apprehension. Revenge was sweet.

"You two." He turned and pointed to Orth and Neeves. "Get on along to the marshal's office, make sure he can't interfere in my business."

The two rogues were followed out

by Pacey and Elgart, who intended keeping an eye on the bank.

Santa Paula's obese and lazy marshal was dozing on the couch in his office when Orth and Neeves marched in. They roused him, but just long enough for him to lurch to his feet, after which Neeves knocked him senseless and toted him into the jailhouse and Orth unhitched the keyring. Luke Deitz was still unconscious when they locked him in a cell.

"Pushover," grinned Orth. "Ain't much of a town, but . . . "

"It's all ours," declared Neeves.

The banker's daughter was now racing her mount northeastward, and coming to grief.

8

Hard Justice

THE mishap was witnessed by six horsemen of whom Davinia was unaware. Through thick grass the filly was running when she balked, startled by a jackrabbit skittering across dry ground a few yards beyond. Davinia, caught by surprise when her mount reared, was thrown. The six promptly changed direction, breaking from the trail, making for the clump of grass.

Stretch captured the filly's rein and began soothing her, while her owner came upright, minus hat and with her dark hair cascading about her shoulders. Larry, Jim and Doc swung down; she flinched from them, crying, "*More* of you . . . ?"

"More of what?" growled Larry.

"No hysterics, if you please," Doc commanded her.

"He's a doctor, young lady, and a good one," said Jim.

"I — don't need a doctor . . . " she faltered, feeling at her ribs, her limbs. "I'm only bruised. The grass cushioned my fall."

"You were ridin' like crazy," said Larry. "Listen, it's okay for you to run scared, but not from *us*, savvy?"

"Seeking help, I presume?" asked Doc.

"Strangers in town — trouble-makers?" demanded Jim. She nodded apprehensively. "Eleven?"

"About that many," she frowned.

"Let's clear the air," said Jim. "We aren't with Mulhauser and his trash. We've been hunting them. So you've nothing to fear from us. Now will you tell us your name? Mine's Gage."

"Vincent Beaumont," offered Doc. "Your servant, young lady."

"He's Emerson, I'm Valentine," said Larry. "Slow Wolf's a good friend of ours. The Mex, we brought him along so Jim'd have somethin' to kick when he gets mad. Who're we talkin' to?"

"Davinia," she said. "Davinia Farwell."

"Farwell!" Jim snapped his fingers. "Now it all fits! You have a bank in Santa Paula? Your father manages it?"

"And he recognized one of those . . ." she began.

"He was chief prosecution witness at Mulhauser's trail," Jim reminded his companions. "I *knew* revenge would be that madman's motive."

"Yeah, you guessed right," agreed Stretch. "And time's a'wastin'."

He handed the filly's rein to Davinia. Larry put a hand on her shoulder and gestured to a copse.

"That's as far as you go, you hearin' me? You head into them trees and wait — and listen. When you can't hear no more shootin', that's when you can head home."

"But not before," stressed Doc.

"You do like I tell you," urged Larry, "and we'll do what we got to do."

"Which'll include lookin' out for your pa," promised Stretch. "Okay?"

He boosted her to her saddle. Watching them remount, she felt hope surge within her. What a mixture they were, these strangers, but resolute and formidable. So there was still hope, and she shouldn't detain them. She redonned her borrowed hat and started for the copse.

From there, she followed the movements of six riders advancing on her hometown's northern outskirts. She had paid little attention to the Indian and the nervous-looking Mexican, the other four having so profoundly impressed her, easing her fears, restoring hope.

The Texans, she was thinking. Two such hard-boiled characters, but kind to her in their own rough way. The elegantly attired one; at first he had seemed somewhat irascible, a man of little patience, but then he had shown her courtesy in the grand manner, making her feel like a lady of distinction. And the big man of sombre demeanor, he who had dismounted from the finest horse she had ever seen, that magnificent black stallion. Her name had stirred him. He must have travelled a great distance, for the incident that had won her father a vengeance-crazed enemy had happened long ago and far away. He knew about it, the man called Gage. He understood.

With the shabby settlement coming into view, Larry reverted to type; he talked battle tactics.

"A line of rock away there left of us — high rocks," he observed. "We're here to stop Mulhauser and his whole bunch, and the wrong way to do that would be to ride in and get shot off of our horses."

"Then we'd be no help to this town, no help at all," drawled Stretch.

"So we walk in," said Larry. "Leave our critters this side of the rocks — and just walk in." He glanced at Jim. "What d'you say?"

"Best way," decided Jim.

"I agree," said Doc. "Eleven aren't too many for us, but why give them any advantage?"

They veered to the rocks, dismounted and ground-reined their animals. Stretch unsheathed his full-loaded Winchester and tossed it to Benito. The little man caught it — reluctantly. Just as reluctantly, Slow Wolf checked his own rifle.

"So much for our plans," he complained to the trouble-shooters. "A few weeks of camping and hunting in the high country."

"Well, you know how it goes, Chief," shrugged Stretch. "We got somethin' a mite more important to tend now."

He, Larry, Jim and Doc drew and checked the loading of their six-shooters. Unnecessary. A reflex action. Re-holstering their pistols, they traded glances.

"It's that time," said Jim.

"Trail's end for you, Gage," nodded Doc.

"Uh huh," grunted Stretch. "So . . . "

"Let's do it," growled Larry.

"Do we have — any strategy?" Slow Wolf asked as they emerged from the rocks.

"Well, when the shootin' starts, we oughtn't stay bunched," opined Larry.

"That would be ill-advised," said Doc.

"We hunt what cover we can find," said Jim. "From then on, every man for himself, each of us concentrating on those trying to put him down."

They moved through brush separating them from Main Street's north end, at which time the wild-eyed one was striding to the centre of the street with his back-ups, all but Pacey and Elgart, now loitering on the sidewalk opposite the bank. The few townfolk in evidence were making themselves scarce, as were the handful of prospectors who had stayed behind after the boom in hopes of picking up the leavings. Small town folk they were, intimidated by this influx of heavily armed strangers and their fearsome leader in particular.

Arms akimbo and facing south, Mulhauser raised his harsh voice. His big moment had come, the moment he had hungered for, nursing his hate and obsession every day of his years of imprisonment.

"I'm here, Reavis Farwell! You know me — and now I'm tellin' you what I'm here for! Today, this town dies — by fire — and any that try to stop us'll die!" He paused as Pacey and Elgart made to cross to the bank. "*You two*!" They froze, listening. "Do what you will, but don't kill the banker! That's to be *my* pleasure!"

From inside the bank, Farwell answered him, making a plea for the town he had striven to keep alive.

"Spare Santa Paula, Mulhauser! Kill me — if that's so important to you — but don't destroy the town and its people!"

Mulhauser's triumphant retort was clearly audible to the other strangers now entering the street from the north. Benito, hugging Stretch's rifle, promptly scuttled away to seek safe refuge.

Cautiously, Slow Wolf began plodding to a horse trough on the street's west side. That left the Texans, Jim and Doc advancing side by side, but with two yards separating each man. From Doc's left hand dangled the headgear one of Mulhauser's followers would recognize, a sweat-stained Stetson with the top of its crown shot through. He swept back his coattails; his right hand brushed the ebony butt of his Colt.

"No mercy, Farwell!" taunted Mulhauser. "For you — *or* the town! I'll have my revenge — *now!*" He growled orders to Brell, Addison and Neeves. "The general store. Fetch coal-oil, all you can find, and douse every building."

Hearing that, the big man from north Nevada decided it was time for him to announce himself.

"Forget it!" Jim called that command grimly. "There'll be no burning here!"

The would-be looters and arsonists stood stock still a long moment. Even before he turned, Mulhauser knew who had challenged them, remembered the voice of the man who had humiliated him in a town far from here. He whirled, gawking at Jim. The other men followed suit and, sighting only four challengers, filled their hands and began scattering, shooting fast at two from Texas, one from New Orleans and one from Nevada, who had emptied their holsters fast.

Doc flung the holed Stetson before following the Texans, who were darting to the east sidewalk. The hat fell in front of the running Willy Stack as his uncle retreated into an alley on the west side with Jim in pursuit. Stack gaped at the hat and reacted fast, swinging his booming Colt to line on Doc.

Doc fired first and Stack reeled and flopped, dropping his gun, grovelling in the dust, pawing at his bloody chest and crying, "Uncle Carl — Uncle Carl . . . !"

Fast on his feet, but too fast with his pistol, Orth triggered at the taller Texan. His bullet missed its moving target by all of three and a half feet, and then Larry's Colt roared and Orth pitched to the dust.

In a matter of moments, there were only two dead invaders in the street. The others had made it to cover and their challengers were doing likewise. Slow Wolf was prone between a water trough and the west sidewalk when Larry, about to follow Stretch and Doc into an alley opening off the east side, spotted the two men dashing for the bank.

"Time for us to split up," he muttered.

"All right, runt," said Stretch. "Till I see you again, watch your butt."

"Count on it," nodded Larry, as he started downtown.

Benito had dived through a window and scared the daylights out of two fellow-Mexicans, one male and aged, the other female, young and plump.

They gaped at him as he came erect. He had eyes only for the full-bosomed young woman; he was smitten.

In his native tongue, he offered a reassurance.

"Do not be afraid. I am Benito Espina, leader of the brave ones who have come to rescue you." With a fine show of bravado, he levered a shell into the breach of Stretch's rifle. "Now you will be safe, for I will protect you — with my life."

Father and daughter mumbled fervent gratitude; he only heard and saw the daughter.

Ears cocked to the intermittent barking of guns, Pacey and the flashy gunslinger checked the locked door of the bank and traded mirthless grins.

"Ain't this pitiful?" commented Pacey. "One kick'll wreck it — and I got me an empty sack."

"So what're we waitin' for?" chuckled Elgart. "Let's *fill* the sack."

With that, he swung a powerful kick at the doorknob. The door burst free of its hinges and toppled inward and he and Pacey followed it with guns drawn, while Larry dashed for the bank's south side, crossing the street as fast as his legs could carry him.

He heard a rifle bark, saw the slug kick up dust inches from his left boot and kept going. Then he was in the alley beside the building and feeling at its plank wall.

Farwell was behind the counter, his hands raised. Pacey tossed the sack to him.

"Gonna make me say it, huh Pop?" he jibed. "Okay, I'll say it. Unlock the safe, fill the sack. Every dime, hear? No stallin'."

"I'll keep an eye on him," muttered Elgart. "You guard the door."

He moved to the counter with his Colt aimed at Farwell, as Pacey retreated to the door. Shrugging helplessly, the banker droped to one knee, produced his keys and fitted one into the safe's lock.

Larry's examination of the south wall

convinced him it was possible; he could do it. The planks were loose and sun-dried, brittle. If he went in this way, and that was his intention, it would be close quarters, but he'd have an edge, the element of surprise.

He retreated a few paces, turned side-on to the wall and charged it left shoulder first, head down. The impact of his heavy body smashed wood; splintered planks gave way and then he was pitching through the opening to flop to the floor. The black-garbed man hefting two six-guns had to be his first target. He triggered, yelling to Farwell to drop, and Elgart lurched drunkenly. He rolled, and not a second too soon. From the doorway, Pacey's gun boomed, the bullet plowing a hole in the floor. Before he could recock, Larry fired again. His bullet hit Pacey dead centre and threw him out to sprawl lifeless on the sidewalk.

Elgart, face contorted, was steadying himself, raising his pistols. Both those weapons were cocked and, with the gunslick less than five feet from him, Larry was loath to take chances. He rose with his Colt roaring and jumping in his fist. Elgart shuddered from the impact and sagged to his knees with his guns discharging, but into the floor. He bowed forward and was dead before his face met the floorboards.

While ejecting spent shells and reloading, Larry growled at the banker.

"Stow the dinero back in the safe later. Stay under cover." He made for the doorway, adding, "And don't fret about your daughter. She's safe."

Warily, his reloaded .45 cocked, he emerged from the bank to scan the street, pausing a moment beside Pacey's body. He couldn't see the rifleman drawing a bead on him, but Slow Wolf did. From behind the trough, his Winchester barked. Larry tensed, raised his eyes and saw Strueby atop the roof of the building opposite, dropping a rifle and following it, nosediving into the street. Dust rose as, head-first, his fall ended.

Twice, while Jim pursued the cursing Mulhauser along a side alley and the area separating westside buildings from the slag heaps, death almost claimed him. The fleeing wild one fired over his shoulder; the bullets came close, and still he followed his quarry.

Mulhauser darted through the rear doorway of a barn, a move not missed by Jim, who kept coming. Now he had a decision to make and realized his life was in the balance. Had Mulhauser quit the barn through the front door, or was he still in here, lying in wait? Should he charge in fully exposed to his enemy, count on out-shooting him with his superior aim and speed, or approach with caution? A sudden mental picture of May and their son demanded he take the latter course.

He sidled to the near edge of the doorway, tugged off his Stetson and inched an eye and half his head around to check the interior. No animals in stalls. The place appeared empty till he squinted up and to his left to the hayloft. Why would straw be dropping between boards of the loft's floor? There was no draft. The straw slipping through those cracks had been disturbed — by a man's weight — a man lying prone, waiting for him to enter.

Fragments fluttered down from that part of the loft just beyond the ladder. As Jim showed himself with his long-barrelled raised and cocked, he was thinking.

"No, Mulhauser. You rate no more chance than you gave Hank."

He aimed for the underside of the hayloft and squeezed trigger and, with the din of the report, heard Mulhauser's animal-like snarl. More straw filtered through the cracks and the hole gouged by the .45 slug as Mulhauser writhed, and then he was visible at the outer edge, half-upright, blood welling from the wound in his midriff, the eyes still as wild, the face a mask of hate — and both hands full of cocked Colt.

Jim fired again. The wild-eyed one

jerked convulsively. His trigger-fingers contracted and, with the roar of the reports, two holes were bored in the south wall. He keeled forward, the weight of his torso taking him over the edge to plunge to the straw-strewn floor.

Though the crumpled figure wasn't moving, Jim recocked and approached it warily. He had almost reached the body when, from behind him, he heard the click of a hammer being thumbed back.

He whirled and fired fast and the man framed in the rear doorway, Addison, died without crying out, hurtling back into the alley with arms out-flung, pistol flying from his hand, and fell spread-eagled.

After that shot echoed, all was quiet, but Stretch's arithmetic didn't fail him. The sudden silence did *not* mean all eleven raiders were accounted for. Some of them still staked out to sneak-shoot at Santa Paula's rescuers. But where? He was in the back alley running parallel with the street on its east side when he asked himself this question.

And not far from the firestairs leading to the upper gallery of the saloon. Inside there maybe? Only one way to find out. He moved along to the stairs and climbed them slowly.

Reaching the gallery, he darted glances north and south along the alley, holstered his matched .45's and moved to a half-open window. When he climbed through, he found himself in the saloon-keeper's bedroom. He crossed it to the door and dropped a hand to the knob. It turned easily. Carefully he opened it and, before stepping into the corridor, drew his Colts again and cocked them. He started for the top of the staircase quietly, ready for anything, including what he saw in the bar-room below upon reaching the balustrade.

In a corner, Neeves was crouched behind an overturned table with a rifle levelled at the batwings. Clark too was visible to Stretch, behind the bar, gripping a shotgun and, like the other man, covering the entrance.

Stretch's righthand Colt was pointed at Neeves, his other Colt at Clark, when he called to them.

"Give up on it. Drop 'em."

As they reached, rising to swing their weapons his way, he squeezed both triggers. Neeves died without firing, his body draped grotesquely over the table's upper edge. Clark reeled while falling, both barrels of the shotgun blasting a hole in the ceiling.

On the street, Doc was treading steadily, warily, his cocked Colt at the ready. An alleymouth dead ahead. He advanced to it stealthily, darted a quick glance along it and saw nothing between him and its rear end. Lady Luck and his sixth sense, however, weren't about to let him down. He began crossing the alleymouth, but still watching its rear end. And then Horrocks appeared there, his Colt belching fire. Doc felt the bullet's hot wind, stood his ground, aimed and fired and saw Horrocks stagger and collapse.

He moved into the alley and all the way to the fallen man. Before turning the body over with a boot, he bent to wrest the gun from the nerveless hand. Horrock's eyes were open, but not seeing him. He grimaced and returned to the alleymouth for a narrow-eyed scan of the street.

Somewhere, a Winchester barked. To impress the senorita he hoped would become his latest conquest, Benito was triggering at imaginary adversaries from the bedroom window.

The woman begged him to be careful.

"When Don Benito defends a woman," he grandly declared, "he cares nothing for his own life."

From just inside the saloon entrance, Stretch bellowed to his cohorts.

"We better do some tallyin'! I see four stiffs in the street! Couple more in here makes six! Runt?"

Larry, hunkered beside Slow Wolf

in a doorway, replied, "Another stiff in the bank!"

"Makes seven," said Stretch. "Jimbo?"

"Two," Jim announced from the barn's street entrance. "Including Mulhauser."

"And one makes ten." Doc sounded disgruntled.

"All right, Number Eleven!" shouted Larry. "You gonna quit — or do it the hard way?"

No answer from Brell, who had broken into the general store from the rear and helped himself to a shotgun and shells. When Strueby had fallen to his death, Brell had lost a relative, his cousin. Now he craved to exact vengeance, to take as many of the rescuers as he could get a bead on. Let them start searching for him; it would cost them. He retreated to the rubble littering the base of a rocky rise beyond the slag heaps west of the settlement, hunkered down, cocked the shotgun and waited his chance.

In the silence, Jim's keen ears had

caught sounds of furtive movement. He moved back through the barn, passing the bodies of Mulhauser and Addison, emerged from its rear exit and made cautiously for the slap heaps. Then he glimpsed Doc disappearing between two of those mounds and quickened his pace.

Hustling to the west side of the mounds, he saw Doc glancing his way — and someone else. Brell had half risen and had the unsuspecting dude in his sights.

"Down, Doc!" he roared, and his Colt boomed twice.

Doc ducked. Brell staggered in his death-throes turning a full circle. The double blast of the scattergun, its muzzles directed at the rockface, was the last sound Brell heard; the weapon slid from his grasp and he slumped against old rubble.

"Typical of you — or those dratted Texans," Doc scowled as he straightened up. "Gage, I believe you *enjoy* putting me in your debt."

"Seemed a good idea at the time," Jim replied with a wry grin. "Larry! Stretch! That was Number Eleven!"

"You hear that, folks?" Larry called to the locals. "It's all over! You can come on out!"

The six victors reassembled and moved downtown to the bank. There, the shaken Reavis Farwell was informed all was well; he could restore the bank's funds to the safe and his unharmed daughter would rejoin him presently.

"Mulhauser — that madman," he sighed. "After all these years." He studied Santa Paula's benefactors dazedly. "How did you come to this place — right when it seemed . . . ?"

"Long story, friend," shrugged Larry. "All you want to know is we were set on stoppin' Mulhauser and his bunch. They caused too much grief, and not just in one place."

"We'll be leaving now," said Jim. "I take it there are enough able-bodied men here to handle the burial chore?"

"They'd have destroyed this town." Farwell showed spirit now. "They'll be buried this very day, but a distance from where our own dead, including my wife, were laid to rest."

Within the hour, Santa Paula was an excited community, and not only because of the bloody battle fought here. By the time Davinia returned, the fever was in the air; she sensed it, for it was one of her childhood memories. The community's handful of prospectors had spread the news. The double blast triggered by the last gunman to die had gouged a chunk out of the rocky slope, revealing what every gold-seeker dreamed of, a rich quartz vein.

The rescuers reflected on the irony of this. Slow Wolf had fetched the horses. They were mounting, all but the runty Mex, who surprised them by declared his intention of prolonging his stay in Santa Paula.

"Why?" Jim asked suspiciously.

"Amor, Amigo Jim," leered Benito.

"Here I have found my true love."

"Again?" scowled Jim.

"Caesar's ghost," exclaimed Doc. "Is there a woman *anywhere* who'd encourage the advances of this buck-toothed little lecher?"

"Seems there's one here," grinned Stretch.

"Wonders will never cease," remarked Slow Wolf.

"I have proven to her I am one valiente caballero," bragged Benito.

"To her," jibed Larry. "Not to us." He had singled out the strawberry roan and now handed its rein to the big man.

"Another gold strike," Jim mused, as he rode north out of Santa Paula with Doc, Slow Wolf and the Texans. "Apparently Farwell's been hoping it'd happen again."

"So it's nice we're gettin' the hell out of this territory," muttered Stretch. "Larry and me, we're leery of boom towns. Too much fever, too much greed for our likin'."

"Ain't that the truth," agreed Larry.

When they reined up a mile from the settlement, Doc made a speech.

"We each had our reasons for regrouping, for involving ourselves in mayhem and bloodshed. Now it's done. A fine horse has been avenged and a band of dangerous homicidal rogues disposed of. It is my fervent hope I'll see none of you again."

"I think Doc's said that before," Stretch remarked to his partner.

"Does sound kind of familiar, yeah," nodded Larry.

"I will now proceed to Denver — alone," announced Doc, "in hopes of encountering fellow sporting men and, of course, enriching myself at their expense."

As he nudged his bay to movement, Slow Wolf raised a hand as though in benediction and intoned, "May the Great Spirit watch over, protect you in time of . . ."

"Amen, Slow Wolf," Doc called over his shoulder.

"Friend Lawrence, friend Woodville . . . " began Slow Wolf.

"You don't have to say it, Chief," Larry assured him. "You still hanker some huntin', but you'd as soon hunt by yourself."

"Nothing personal — please do not be offended," said Slow Wolf. "Always a pleasure being reunited with you, but such reunions invariably . . . "

"Sure," nodded Stretch. "You sided with us in another ruckus, but you didn't enjoy it none. We savvy. Good huntin', Chief."

The pudgy half-breed shook hands with the Texans and the man from Nevada and idled his dun away in the general direction of the high country, leaving three tough veterans to trade long looks.

"I intend heading home by way of Sawyerville," offered Jim. "I can wire May from there, and Sheriff Ilford ought to be told Mulhauser'll cause no more misery. I'll also return this stolen horse. You fiddlefoots're welcome to ride along with me — all the way. Hospitality aplenty for you at my spread, stay as long as you wish, rest yourselves."

"We sure appreciate the invite, Jim," said Larry. "But it'd be a dirty trick on your wife and kid. And you know that for a fact. *No* place stays peaceful after we show up."

"We don't savvy why, but that's how it goes," shrugged Stretch.

"Whatever you say," agreed Jim, offering his hand. "Quite a party this was, huh?" As the drifters shook with him, he suggested, "Let's call this hasta la vista, not adios. Because, as you'd say, Larry, I have a feeling in my bones that says our trails'll cross again."

"It's a big country, big feller, but a small world," grinned Larry. He and Stretch sat their mounts, staring after the man on the handsome black stallion till they could see only his dust. "I'm glad Jim's all settled down with a family and his own spread."

"Uh huh," grunted Stretch. "Couldn't

happen to a better man than him. So — uh — you want to ride a wide circle round Santa Paula, head for New Mexico maybe?"

"We'll do that, sure," said Larry. "Might be quieter for us down there."

"*That'll* be the day," sighed Stretch.

"We can always hope," shrugged Larry.

THE END

Books by Marshall Grover
in the Linford Western Library:

BANDIT BAIT
EMERSON'S HIDEOUT
HEROES AND HELLERS
GHOST-WOMAN OF CASTILLO
THE DEVIL'S DOZEN
HELL IN HIGH COUNTRY
TEN FAST HORSES
SAVE A BULLET FOR KEEHOE
DANGER RODE DRAG
THE KILLERS WORE BLACK
REUNION IN SAN JOSE
CORMACK CAME BACK
RESCUE PARTY
KINCAID'S LAST RIDE
7 FOR BANNER PASS
THE HELLION BREED
THE TRUTH ABOUT SNAKE RIDGE
DEVIL'S DINERO
HARTIGAN
SHOTGUN SHARKEY
THE LOGANTOWN LOOTERS
THE SEVENTH GUILTY MAN
BULLET FOR A WIDOW

CALABOOSE EXPRESS
WHISKEY GULCH
THE ALIBI TRAIL
SIX GUILTY MEN
FORT DILLON
IN PURSUIT OF QUINCEY BUDD
HAMMER'S HORDE
TWO GENTLEMEN FROM TEXAS
HARRIGAN'S STAR
TURN THE KEY ON EMERSON
ROUGH ROUTE TO RODD COUNTY
SEVEN KILLERS EAST
DAKOTA DEATH-TRAP
GOLD, GUNS & THE GIRL
RUCKUS AT GILA WELLS
LEGEND OF COYOTE FORD

Other titles in the Linford Western Library:

TOP HAND
Wade Everett

The Broken T was big. But no ranch is big enough to let a man hide from himself.

GUN WOLVES OF LOBO BASIN
Lee Floren

The Feud was a blood debt. When Smoke Talbot found the outlaws who gunned down his folks he aimed to nail their hide to the barn door.

SHOTGUN SHARKEY
Marshall Grover

The westbound coach carrying the indomitable Larry and Stretch headed for a shooting showdown.

FIGHTING RAMROD
Charles N. Heckelmann

Most men would have cut their losses, but Frazer counted the bullets in his guns and said he'd soak the range in blood before he'd give up another inch of what was his.

LONE GUN
Eric Allen

Smoke Blackbird had been away too long. The Lequires had seized the Blackbird farm, forcing the Indians and settlers off, and no one seemed willing to fight! He had to fight alone.

THE THIRD RIDER
Barry Cord

Mel Rawlins wasn't going to let anything stand in his way. His father was murdered, his two brothers gone. Now Mel rode for vengeance.

ARIZONA DRIFTERS
W. C. Tuttle

When drifting Dutton and Lonnie Steelman decide to become partners they find that they have a common enemy in the formidable Thurston brothers.

TOMBSTONE
Matt Braun

Wells Fargo paid Luke Starbuck to outgun the silver-thieving stagecoach gang at Tombstone. Before long Luke can see the only thing bearing fruit in this eldorado will be the gallows tree.

HIGH BORDER RIDERS
Lee Floren

Buckshot McKee and Tortilla Joe cut the trail of a border tough who was running Mexican beef into Texas. They stopped the smuggler in his tracks.

BRETT RANDALL, GAMBLER
E. B. Mann

Larry Day had the choice of running away from the law or of assuming a dead man's place. No matter what he decided he was bound to end up dead.

THE GUNSHARP
William R. Cox

The Eggerleys weren't very smart. They trained their sights on Will Carney and Arizona's biggest blood bath began.

THE DEPUTY OF SAN RIANO
Lawrence A. Keating and Al. P. Nelson

When a man fell dead from his horse, Ed Grant was spotted riding away from the scene. The deputy sheriff rode out after him and came up against everything from gunfire to dynamite.

FARGO: MASSACRE RIVER
John Benteen

The ambushers up ahead had now blocked the road. Fargo's convoy was a jumble, a perfect target for the insurgents' weapons!

SUNDANCE: DEATH IN THE LAVA
John Benteen

The Modoc's captured the wagon train and its cargo of gold. But now the halfbreed they called Sundance was going after it . . .

HARSH RECKONING
Phil Ketchum

Five years of keeping himself alive in a brutal prison had made Brand tough and careless about who he gunned down . . .

FARGO: PANAMA GOLD
John Benteen

With foreign money behind him, Buckner was going to destroy the Panama Canal before it could be completed. Fargo's job was to stop Buckner.

FARGO: THE SHARPSHOOTERS
John Benteen

The Canfield clan, thirty strong were raising hell in Texas. Fargo was tough enough to hold his own against the whole clan.

PISTOL LAW
Paul Evan Lehman

Lance Jones came back to Mustang for just one thing — revenge! Revenge on the people who had him thrown in jail.

HELL RIDERS
Steve Mensing

Wade Walker's kid brother, Duane, was locked up in the Silver City jail facing a rope at dawn. Wade was a ruthless outlaw, but he was smart, and he had vowed to have his brother out of jail before morning!

DESERT OF THE DAMNED
Nelson Nye

The law was after him for the murder of a marshal — a murder he didn't commit. Breen was after him for revenge — and Breen wouldn't stop at anything . . . blackmail, a frameup . . . or murder.

DAY OF THE COMANCHEROS
Steven C. Lawrence

Their very name struck terror into men's hearts — the Comancheros, a savage army of cutthroats who swept across Texas, leaving behind a bloodstained trail of robbery and murder.

SUNDANCE: SILENT ENEMY
John Benteen

A lone crazed Cheyenne was on a personal war path. They needed to pit one man against one crazed Indian. That man was Sundance.

LASSITER
Jack Slade

Lassiter wasn't the kind of man to listen to reason. Cross him once and he'll hold a grudge for years to come — if he let you live that long.

LAST STAGE TO GOMORRAH
Barry Cord

Jeff Carter, tough ex-riverboat gambler, now had himself a horse ranch that kept him free from gunfights and card games. Until Sturvesant of Wells Fargo showed up.

McALLISTER ON THE COMANCHE CROSSING
Matt Chisholm

The Comanche, McAllister owes them a life — and the trail is soaked with the blood of the men who had tried to outrun them before.

QUICK-TRIGGER COUNTRY
Clem Colt

Turkey Red hooked up with Curly Bill Graham's outlaw crew. But wholesale murder was out of Turk's line, so when range war flared he bucked the whole border gang alone . . .

CAMPAIGNING
Jim Miller

Ambushed on the Santa Fe trail, Sean Callahan is saved by two Indian strangers. But there'll be more lead and arrows flying before the band join Kit Carson against the Comanches.

GUNSLINGER'S RANGE
Jackson Cole

Three escaped convicts are out for revenge. They won't rest until they put a bullet through the head of the dirty snake who locked them behind bars.

RUSTLER'S TRAIL
Lee Floren

Jim Carlin knew he would have to stand up and fight because he had staked his claim right in the middle of Big Ike Outland's best grass.

THE TRUTH ABOUT SNAKE RIDGE
Marshall Grover

The troubleshooters came to San Cristobal to help the needy. For Larry and Stretch the turmoil began with a brawl and then an ambush.

WOLF DOG RANGE
Lee Floren

Will Ardery would stop at nothing, unless something stopped him first — like a bullet from Pete Manly's gun.

DEVIL'S DINERO
Marshall Grover

Plagued by remorse, a rich old reprobate hired the Texas Troubleshooters to deliver a fortune in greenbacks to each of his victims.

GUNS OF FURY
Ernest Haycox

Dane Starr, alias Dan Smith, wanted to close the door on his past and hang up his guns, but people wouldn't let him.

DONOVAN
Elmer Kelton

Donovan was supposed to be dead. Uncle Joe Vickers had fired off both barrels of a shotgun into the vicious outlaw's face as he was escaping from jail. Now Uncle Joe had been shot — in just the same way.

CODE OF THE GUN
Gordon D. Shirreffs

MacLean came riding home, with saddle tramp written all over him, but sewn in his shirt-lining was an Arizona Ranger's star.

GAMBLER'S GUN LUCK
Brett Austen

Gamblers seldom live long. Parker was a hell of a gambler. It was his life — or his death . . .

ORPHAN'S PREFERRED
Jim Miller

Sean Callahan answers the call of the Pony Express and fights Indians and outlaws to get the mail through.

DAY OF THE BUZZARD
T. V. Olsen

All Val Penmark cared about was getting the men who killed his wife.

THE MANHUNTER
Gordon D. Shirreffs

Lee Kershaw knew that every Rurale in the territory was on the lookout for him. But the offer of $5,000 in gold to find five small pieces of leather was too good to turn down.

RIFLES ON THE RANGE
Lee Floren

Doc Mike and the farmer stood there alone between Smith and Watson. There was this moment of stillness, and then the roar would start. And somebody would die . . .

HARTIGAN
Marshall Grover

Hartigan had come to Cornerstone to die. He chose the time and the place, and Main Street became a battlefield.

SUNDANCE: OVERKILL
John Benteen

When a wealthy banker's daughter was kidnapped by the Cheyenne, he offered Sundance $10,000 to rescue the girl.

RIDE A LONE TRAIL
Gordon D. Shirreffs

The valley was about to explode into open range war. All it needed was the fuse and Ken Macklin was it.

HARD MAN WITH A GUN
Charles N. Heckelmann

After Bob Keegan lost the girl he loved and the ranch he had sweated blood to build, he had nothing left but his guts and his guns but he figured that was enough.

SUNDANCE: IRON MEN
Peter McCurtin

Sundance, assigned to save the railroad from a murder spree, soon came to realise that he'd have to fight fire with fire, bullets with bullets and death with death!